The Liberated

Brittiany West

This is a work of fiction. All characters and events portrayed in this book are fictitious.

THE LIBERATED

2015 © by Brittiany West

All rights reserved, including the right to reproduce or copy this content or any portion thereof.

Cover design by Brittiany West

To Mom and Dad,
Thank you for raising me in such a wonderful place where my imagination could take off, and for appeasing my insatiable appetite for books.

And to all my wonderful teachers throughout the years, thank you for nurturing my love of writing.

"…and so you ran, on towards a new life…

…you were awakened by your ambition, to be free and run your own course…

…and while the path is unknown and the future remains unclear, one thing is for certain…

…man is free at the moment he wishes to be…"

-Voltaire

Prologue

I sat very still, feeling as if I'd been slapped.

"She wants you to do *what?*" I spluttered. This couldn't be happening. I wouldn't let it happen. I stood up and began to pace, shaking my head, willing the words I'd just heard to get out of my head. Maybe it was denial.

Wes sighed uncomfortably and leaned against the cold tile wall.

"It's just for a month or so, Lily," he replied quietly. "There's very little danger since we'll be cutting through the forest towards the border. We won't even be near the city. I'll be back before you know it."

"I didn't ask how long it was going to be," I snapped. "Why is she sending you?"

"Because I'm familiar with the area and I know people there. If we can gather a force down there to come up against the city, then-"

"She's sending you because she hates me."

Wes rolled his eyes. "Since when did you get so paranoid?"

"It's not paranoia, it's the truth! She's done nothing but treat me like crap since we got here!"

My voice rose hysterically. I knew mom could probably hear us from the little bedroom she and I shared down the hall, but I didn't care.

"Well, you haven't exactly been nice to her either," he said quietly.

He cringed when I kicked the wall, leaving a small crack in the ceramic. My strength had increased lately for some reason. I cursed inwardly. Now even Wes thought I was a freak.

"Fine, Wes. Go have your little adventure, go be the hero while I sit here, husking corn and slowly rotting."

"Lily, I don't even leave until tomorrow evening! Let's not ruin the last few hours we have together!"

Tears came unbidden, making my face grow hot with shame. Since when had I become so emotionally dependent on a guy? But Wes wasn't just any guy, and now he wanted to leave. Aching and confused, I turned and walked off down the hall, ignoring his pleas.

"Fine!" he hollered, his voice rising with anger. "I thought maybe just once you could muster it together to be supportive, to recognize how scared I am to have to do this and encourage me after *all* I've done for you, but I guess that's too much to ask! You expect me to be at your beck and call, making sure you're not traumatized or hurt, not even caring what I've been through or what I have to go through now!"

Ouch. That stung. I whirled around, my tears burning and choking my throat as I gasped out a reply.

"I've had to do quite a lot without depending on you, *Wesley*," I shot back witheringly, enjoying the look he got on his face at the use of his full name. "And for your information, I worried about you every single day when you got drafted. The guilt was horrible, knowing it was my fault that you got captured and sent to the front. And now, I get to feel that all over again while you make me out to be the villain and tell me how unsupportive I am."

He sighed and curled his fist against the wall. "Lily, that's not it at all…"

"Just save it!" I yelled, not caring anymore who heard me. "I don't want to hear about it anymore! I hope you make it back, but don't expect me to be there goggling over you like an idiot!"

I turned and kept walking, barging loudly into the little bedroom, feeling strangely empty and numb. Mom sat huddled on one of the small beds, pretending to read a book.

"Sorry for the noise, mom," I rasped through a fresh wave of tears. She didn't say anything. She simply got up from her bed, walked over and wrapped her arms around me. The tears came more heavily then, heaving my whole body.

Questions flitted through my mind. Had we broken up? Was it really that impossible for us to weather one fight? Then again, our relationship had never exactly been normal. Out of the five months we'd been together, half of those had been spent apart or on the run from the Mainframe.

After a while, I broke away from mom's gentle hold and sat down on my own bed, exhausted. Mom sat next to me and gently stroked my hair.

"Do you want to talk about it?"

I shrugged. "What's to talk about? For once, we can finally just be together without running for our lives and he up and takes this stupid assignment. He just wants to look good for our stupid commander."

"Well…he is the best qualified for this particular job," she began gently. "The southern province could be a huge help turning the tide in the war, and if he already knows people there…"

She trailed off at the look on my face and folded her hands in her lap. I knew she was right, but I didn't want to admit it just now. Or ever.

"I'm sick of this stupid war," I complained. "I just want my old life back, even if living in the city was awful. At least life wasn't so complicated then."

Mom brushed my hair off my face, looking thoughtful. "The war started because a lot of people do want a normal, less complicated life, one that's not threatened at every turn. You know what it's been like in the clutches of the Mainframe. You of all people should know how important it is to stop Vic, to win the war, to turn the tide. Wes understands that, honey. That's why he's leaving. He's not doing it to make himself look good. He's not doing it to spite you. He's doing it for a better life. Because he loves you. I think, deep down, you know that."

I wanted to get mad, to yell back at her, but I couldn't. I knew she was right, as always, but it didn't change the situation or make it better.

Somehow, I managed a few hours of sleep, but the next day still came way too soon. I watched numbly as Wes gathered his things in the main hall and got fitted with some kind of bracelet. He glanced my way more than once, but I stubbornly avoided his looks. A funny little pain began to grow in my heart as I watched him. Half of me wanted desperately to fling myself onto him and beg him never to leave, but my stubborn half won out. I still felt a little convinced that he was fulfilling this mission for the honor, for something to do besides husk corn all day.

I left before he was assigned to a team, unable to face him after the previous night.

Later, I sat in my room, staring at the wall and wishing it had a window. A soft knock sounded at the door.

"You don't have to knock, mom." Sometimes she knocked if she thought I was getting dressed. It was probably a smart idea, considering how many people in the rebellion walked down our hall every day, but it did get a little wearing. We had a little curtained off area where I could hide should she barge in while I was in the middle of a change.

"It's me."

Wes. I took a deep, shuddering breath, willing myself not to cry. I didn't answer, not knowing what to say, so he stepped in anyway.

"Hi."

"Hi," I replied softly.

He knelt down in front of me. "I did want to say goodbye, at least."

"Goodbye."

"Lily…"

For a moment, I felt just like I had that night on the pier when he'd first kissed me, resistant, yet wanting him with all my heart. I clung to that feeling, willing it to stay, but it slipped away as easily as it had come. Wes was still leaving, and nothing could change that.

"I'm sorry, Wes, for the things I said," I mumbled. "But I wish you could understand where I'm coming from. I hate…I can't be without you. It hurts."

He looked around the room, seeming lost. "I'm sorry, too, Lily," he sighed. "It hurts me too, more than you know. But it's something I have to do."

"Why?" I spluttered angrily, feeling the tears coming on again.

He ran a hand through his curly hair. "Because I just…have to."

I turned away from the hand he reached out to me, feeling bitter anger rise up inside me again.

"Well…good luck, then," I snapped. "I hope you become the hero of the rebellion."

"Lily, please-"

"Just go."

His hands twisted themselves together, a habit that always showed up when he was nervous or upset. I watched as he bit his lip, presumably trying to figure out what to say. I knew I should help him out, be supportive, whatever, but I couldn't.

Finally, he stood, clapped me gently on the shoulder and headed for the door.

"I'll see you soon," he whispered. He paused by the door and looked back one last time.

"I still love you, Lily."

After a stony silence, he closed the door gently and was gone. I collapsed on my bed and began to sob.

__Chapter One__

The longest day in history had at last come to an end. I sank down onto the rocky cliffs that overlooked the ocean, took a deep breath and tried to force the tension from my shoulders. My eyes ached from squinting against the sun, waiting, watching, preparing for the worst.

The endless water stretched out before me, a huge, gray undulating blanket reaching out to touch the sinking red sun. The sound of the crashing waves pulling against the velvet sand soothed me, reminding me of better times. I pulled my tatty old coat more tightly around my shoulders, shivering against the cold. Though I loved the northern country, I didn't think I would ever get accustomed to the sharp air. I'd hardly ever needed a coat in the south. November had crept in suddenly, quietly, like a thief in the night, bringing with it one of the worst early winter chills experienced in this part of the country.

As if in a movie, the events of the last few months flashed through my mind again, as it did at the end of every day; our narrow escape from Vic, reaching the northern border just before it closed, Aggs' official funeral, the discovery of the Underground and their headquarters and the commencement of Wes's mission. The leaders of the rebellion tried to comfort me by saying that the Mainframe had mostly withdrawn from Epirus to focus on the rebellion. Supposedly it would make it easier for Wes and his team to cross the border. He'd already been gone two weeks. I felt numb every time I thought about our last encounter, and uneasy that he wouldn't come back. Time had allowed me to heal a little, helping me see just how awful I'd been. Painful guilt over the whole thing constantly boiled inside me, but a tiny sliver of pride wouldn't let me let it go.

It all led up to today, sitting here on the cliffs, bone tired and about to drop. Our spies down south had heard rumors of a possible bombing tonight. We'd fortified our cliff-side fortress, evacuated and secured local residents and gathered enough food to feed the masses for a few days. The fortress had been used in older times during other wars, but had been since abandoned for safety reasons. The rebellion found it and did some work to the structure to make it more sound.

My red, raw hands ached from shucking the last of the fall harvest of corn. Thank goodness that stupid chore was over. If I ever saw another cob of corn, I'd decided I'd spit on it and then heave it into the ocean.

Other rebels had traveled out to the larger cities like Parthin, warning the citizens there to take cover or leave. I thought of Cherie and Crystal, who were now students and roommates at the University in Parthin, according to their last email months ago, and wondered despairingly if they'd be safe.

I settled deeper into a small niche and leaned against the cold rocks, my head on a patch of moss, and closed my eyes. The crashing waves and warmth of my heavy coat soon lulled me to sleep.

I woke sometime later, my joints stiff, my limbs numb and my ears alert. Something felt wrong.

I sat up and rubbed the bleariness from my eyes, trying to figure out what happened. I couldn't seem to hear the sound of the waves crashing against the shore. The sun had long set, leaving a scattering of stars in its wake. An eerie humming sound, faint but loud enough to drown out the waves below, reached my ears. It grew louder by the second. It sounded familiar, but I couldn't quite place it.

Then, fear like I'd never felt suddenly gripped me as I remembered the warnings from earlier in the day, the masses of people huddled underground waiting for the raid, for the bombers. This was it. They were coming. And I'd been stupid enough to use the small set of stairs I'd found in the halls to come hide here, aboveground, a target for all to see. I noticed that thankfully that my coat was the same dull shade of brown as the rocks around me, but it wouldn't help much if they decided to drop the bomb here.

Frantic, I looked back to the small opening in the rocks marked by a boulder with what looked like a huge nose. It was the opening back into the tunnels, the Underground Headquarters, but it was much too far away. They'd probably sealed off the stairs to discourage anyone from coming up here, or perhaps to keep debris from getting in.

I glanced up and noticed the starts blotted out by several curious shapes. The bombers always used InvisiJets, but you could still vaguely see the blurred impression they made against the sky. I knew now that even if the aboveground entrance to HQ wasn't sealed, I wouldn't have enough time now to make it back.

I looked behind me at the ocean and got a sudden idea. Quickly, I crept over to the edge and looked down. It was at least a thirty feet to the surface of the water. I'd gone cliff diving down south with friends before, but we'd always gone low, no more than twenty feet. I wasn't familiar with the area, and had no idea how deep the water was.

I looked back and choked in terror to see that the InvisiJets had already come much closer. Traveling at Mach speed, they could go pretty fast. A cloud suddenly plumed a couple miles away, bright orange against the blackened night. Even from that far away, I felt the air whoosh over me from the impact. I had seconds. They'd already begun. It was either risk the water or be vaporized by an Akrium bomb. With a running start, I flung myself from the cliff towards the turbulent ocean, trying to remember to keep my body rigid and go in feet first.

I screamed in pain as my body smacked the roiling waves. My arms flew out and slapped the surface, creating what I knew would later be a stinging rash, if not welts. My back arched weirdly and twisted, shooting a flash of pain up my spine. The water froze and compacted around my body, turning my clothes into leaden, frozen weights.

At long last, I broke the surface and gulped cold air into my lungs. As the water cleared from my eyes, I noticed I'd started drifting out to sea. Summoning my beastly freak strength, I swam against the current, but one arm seemed to not notice the commands from my brain to move. Grimacing in pain, I used my other arm to lift it above the water. White hot agony shot through the arm from my shoulder to the tips of my fingers. I'd probably broken it in the fall.

I gulped back my tears and headed for shore as best I could with one arm. I finally got clear of the current and felt sand beneath my feet. The shore had been closer than I thought. The waves pushed me gently up the sand until I could crawl onto my feet and reach solid ground. I collapsed as another huge, resounding boom echoed all around me, deafening me and striking fear into my heart once again. I rolled over on my back and saw a strange wave of some kind of smoke rolling off the cliffs towards me, but I was too weak and exhausted to move. Great. Not only had they bombed us, they were gassing us as well. Probably the stuff they'd used in the city that made your eyes bleed. With one last burst of energy, I put my sopping coat sleeve over my nose and mouth and passed out.

- 8 -

Chapter Two

"Are you kidding me?"

The voice cut sharply through my hazy thoughts, slowly bringing me out of my stupor.

"I swear, Lily, if I have to save your butt one more time…"

Someone pushed their cold, bony hands under my back and pushed me up. I screamed out as pain ripped through my arm. Everything suddenly came back in an intense blur of images; the Invisijets flying through the air, my wild leap into oblivion, smacking against the icy water, my arm…

"What is wrong with you?"

Avery. The speaker's voice finally registered in my waterlogged head. How had she gotten here? I blearily opened my eyes and looked around. Dark clouds hovered above me, threatening to spill their contents down on my already freezing body. A strange, foggy cloud hovered above us, pressing down faster with each passing second. Avery stared down at me, her hair wilder than usual, flying out in all directions like some kind of possessed lion.

"Get up!" she hissed.

"My arm…" I groaned, still feeling the knife-like pain shooting up and down my bad limb.

"You don't understand-"

CRACK. My wet hair suddenly felt odd, like it was filled with tiny bubbles or something. And then it hit me. Lightning. The air was filled with an eerie electric charge, the kind that comes when lightning is very nearby. Wow. Bombs, lightning, poison gas…what next? I almost wanted to laugh at it all.

"GET UP!" Avery screamed against the wind. I stumbled to my feet, wincing as my arm jostled around. With one last tug from Avery, I managed to follow her to a small fissure in the cliff face nearby, not a second too late. We climbed in as a huge bolt of lighting struck the sand near the place where I'd been lying. A wave of nausea overtook me suddenly, but Avery didn't allow for any stops. We had to get in before we were seen, bombed, poisoned or electrocuted.

I straggled wearily after Avery, trying to squeeze through the narrow tunnel behind her and keep within the small range of her flashlight. My fingers brushed the rock wall, but oddly the pain had ebbed a bit. It still hurt, just not as intensely, so I nestled my arm into the crook of my other arm and hobbled quickly to keep up.

After a series of twists and turns, we finally came to a flat expanse of rock, or what looked like rock anyway. Avery fumbled along the wall until she found the spot she was looking for. With a light push from her, we were in.

Bright, fluorescent lights blinded me after the dimness of the outer cave. I squinted hard, waiting for my eyes to adjust to the sudden intensity. Footsteps clacked loudly towards us, and I knew without being told who was coming.

"Where was she this time?" demanded a sharp, nasal voice.

"I found her on the beach," Avery replied. "Something's wrong with her arm."

"Get her to the infirmary, then," the voice snapped. Inwardly, I fumed. I hated the nasaly voice, the loud clackety shoes and the snippy attitude, but mostly I hated who they belonged to. Delaney Capell, our "bold" leader, the one who'd known about the small series of tunnels in the sea cliffs and created the base for the rebels.

I felt Avery gently grab my good arm and lead me. As my eyes finally adjusted to the light, I watched the retreating figure of Capell for a moment. She was thin, built like a wire, with blonde and gray hair that looked just as wiry as her figure. Everything about her was calculated and precise, even down to her immaculately hemmed commander pants. Ever since I'd come here, she had treated me like a plague.

"Come on," Avery said wearily. I followed her, one eye still on Capell. I couldn't figure out why, but something about the woman just rubbed me the wrong way. I knew I'd feel that way even if she'd greeted me with milk and cookies.

Through another complicated set of tunnels lay a small room used for the infirmary. Contrary to Capell, Evan, the rebel doctor, was kind and gentle. Considering my accident prone nature, I'd spent a lot of time getting to know him. He was an older guy with twinkly blue eyes and a fuzzy brown ring around his head. He had more hair in his bristly gray mustache than he did up top. The mustache tended to wiggle every time he concentrated hard. He was much less brisk and much more friendly than the others.

"Uh oh," he said in his boisterous voice. "What now, Mitchell?"

"Busted my arm pretty good," I replied.

"Patch her up, will you, Evan?" Avery asked in a voice of exaggerated exasperation. "She can't seem to keep out of here for more than two seconds."

"I'm not complaining," he countered. "You're good company, Mitch." Evan liked nicknames, and he liked to shorten them down. He always called me Mitch.

"I'll see you later," Avery muttered with a good natured wink at me. "Stay outta trouble, ok?"

"Yeah," I replied. I watched her go, her wild hair still flying, and felt a bitter edge enter my thoughts. She, too, had been taken in by Capell. They'd found out her skill with plants and herbal remedies and snatched her up to do research for the cause. She and Trent worked closely together now, using their combined skills to create cures for everything from colds to designing an imitation Akrium cure. Their marriage seemed much better these days, much less formal.

My bitterness was soon overwhelmed by loneliness when I realized how truly much I missed Avery's companionship.

"Let's take a look," said Evan as soon as Avery left. He gently took my hand and extended my arm, frowning as I flinched. He strode to his small desk and took out a mini X-ray. As he waited for the machine to reach full power, he smiled.

"You know, you do come in here a lot, but I like talking to you," he said with his contagious smile. "Don't worry about the others teasing you."

"Thanks, Evan. Feeling's mutual. You're the only non-robot in this place."

"Yeah, well, rebellions tend to make people touchy. I try not to let it get to me."

I laughed, something I rarely did these days. It was impossible not to like Evan's casual sense of humor. I almost wished they'd assign me here as his assistant, but I had no clue about medicine. Besides, my klutzy accidents would probably get someone killed.

"Well, it's busted, alright, but not as badly as I would expect," he sighed after taking the X-ray. "We'll have to get a cast on it. What did you do to it, anyway?"

I paused, not sure if I really wanted to say. "I uh…had a nasty brush out on the water."

"You were swimming?" Evan's furry eyebrows shot up. "In this weather? In *that* water?"

I nodded, glad he didn't press for more details. "Well, Mitch, if I didn't know any better, I'd say you had a death wish."

I shrugged. With Wes gone, sometimes I felt like there was nothing to live for.

Ugh. How had I gone from independent woman of the world to gaga over some guy in a matter of months? Then again, Wes wasn't every guy. I felt a sharp pang of fear shoot through my stomach, making me ill. The tiny voice of doubt whispered disparaging thoughts, musings about Wes's safety in what was previously war-torn country. The fact that the Southern Province wasn't a target anymore didn't really help.

BOOM.

I instinctively clutched my heart and began to gasp. I knew the sounds, and I knew we were okay, but the feeling of panic always took me when the bombs dropped.

"It's ok, Mitch. These tunnels have seen a lot worse than that."

I nodded silently, feeling stupid for showing my fear in front of Evan.

BOOM.

The bombs always went off in the general area. The Mainframe had a vague idea of our whereabouts, but the lack of history lessons in schools had paid off. Since much of the learning was propaganda about the Mainframe, most people had long forgotten the exact location of the tunnels. The nearest town had been abandoned long ago for some reason or another.

"Well, you need a cast and a sling," said Evan, remaining calm and cool despite the fact that small bits of debris shook off from the ceiling and coated everything like dust. "I'm sure that much was obvious. It's a slight fracture."

I breathed a low sigh of relief. I could thank my freak powers for that. Hitting the water at that speed should have cracked my arm in half. Maybe it had, and then healed. Being a mutant did have an upside. With all the accidents I had, it was nice to have rapid healing powers.

BOOM.

"Well, by my calculations, that should be the last one," said Evan gently, noticing that my breathing still hadn't slowed. "Those things are expensive, and they're running out of 'em. Chin up. Let me see your arm so I can get this thing set."

I nodded, worried my voice would tremble and betray the fear I still felt.

"All right, go on then."

Evan gathered his supplies and began work. "This isn't the best time to break your arm, you know," he said, glancing at me furtively.

"Why? I know Capell'll be all over me about not being able to shuck corn, but..."

"No, it's not that," he replied. "Word is that the Council wants to see you."

I looked up from Evan's careful bandaging, surprised. "Why?"

"Dunno. Just said they needed to see you is all."

I lapsed into silence, pondering this latest. It was no secret that Capell didn't like me. We'd come in from the train station, led by an insurgent who'd met us, filthy and tired and hungry. After a brief burial for Aggs, we'd been shunted into this place under cover of night. It was harder for bombers in the Invisijets to see us in the dark. Capell had read all about me on her stolen communicator with the disconnected channel, seen all the warrants for my arrest, the increasing prices on my head. She made it clear from day one that she thought I was some stupid, foolhardy teenager. And yet, I knew without a shadow of a doubt that she was also afraid of me. Sometimes I flexed slightly in boring meetings just to watch her twitch. She knew all about my freak powers now that Vic and the rest of his drones had gotten hold of the cure and started boasting about their super-army that would take down the rebellion. I wondered if she thought I was some kind of double agent.

Yeah, like I could handle that.

Wes, however, was a different story. Capell liked him immediately. She'd offered him the peace-making mission to the Southern Province since he'd made friends there, and he'd accepted it as quickly as she'd offered it. He knew I was mad about it, and just kept saying something about making amends. Wes wouldn't do something crazy without thinking it through, and I'd known he had a good reason to go back, but it still didn't make it any easier. My heart ached without him, and my loneliness grew slowly into bitterness. Even Mom was away a lot. They'd given her assignments in farming and food production, since she'd always been good at gardening and that kind of thing, having grown up where she could have a farm. I thought back to her flower boxes on the windowsills of our cruddy little apartment and wanted to cry.

Though I knew I acted like a spoiled child sometimes, I couldn't help it. With all the horrendous things I'd been through over the summer, it would have been nice to have some kind of support network, but Capell made sure that was all yanked out from under me. Avery was distant now too, keeping up her herbal medicinal work within the base. Her remedies came in handy, since no one else really knew as much about plants as she did. Everyone thrived in the caves, everyone had a purpose.

Except me.

Capell filled my days with meaningless, menial labor until I felt like I would rip my hair out and scream.

"Mitch?"

I looked up, wrenched out of my daze by Evan's warm voice. "You're all set. Just try to keep it still, and don't get it wet."

I nodded. "Thanks. I'm gonna hit the hay, I'm wiped."

"Sleep is the best medicine," he replied, using one of his many adages. I stumbled away from the room, grabbing one of the free-hanging lanterns on my way out. Mom and I were just a few dozen yards from the infirmary.

Mom was already passed out on her mattress. They probably hadn't woken her because she was so used to hearing I was in the infirmary. A wave of sudden sadness washed over me and, rather than fighting it, I let myself sink into it. Tears crept down my cheeks as I lay on my scratchy mattress, trickling into my ears, but I didn't bother to wipe them away. My arm stuck out at an odd angle, forced into a square by my cast, making sleep uncomfortable. As I sank farther beneath the blankets, however, my eyes grew so heavy that I barely had time to think.

Before I sank under, I rubbed the small charm on the necklace around my neck. A cup. The symbol in the Mainframe flag for plenty. The south was always represented by a shield, since the south had always produced superior weapons. The north, with its lush green fields, had always been known for bounteous harvests. The shield and the cup together were crowned with laurel leaves, for victory. I'd never known any of this until I came here, when Capell briefed all the new people and gave us the cup necklaces. They were identifiers, so we knew who were our fellow rebels. I yawned and turned over, still fingering the little cup.

- 14 -

What did Capell want with me? Why would she all of a sudden take an interest? My thoughts drifted into troubled dreams, keeping me in a half-slumber the rest of the night.

Chapter Three

"Honey?"

I woke in the dim light of our cave to see mom hovering over me.

"What did you do to your arm?"

"Fracture," I mumbled.

"Why didn't they wake me?" I could see her going into full mom panic mode, so I sat up and put my good arm reassuringly around her. She had been extra protective of me lately.

"Calm down, it'll heal soon. You know how I am."

"What were you doing?"

I gave her a slightly twisted grin. "Swimming."

"Lily Annabelle…"

Uh oh. My middle name. That was never good.

"How many times have I told you to stay in the caves? You could have drowned! Everyone's saying there was a big storm last night, if I had a penny for every single gray hair you've put on my head…"

I let her go on, not really listening. My main concern was breakfast, and to my delight I noticed that mom had nabbed us a couple plates of pancakes. The work was terrible in this pit, but at least the food was good.

I shoved the food in my mouth at an alarming rate, listening to mom now nagging me about eating like a horse. The food felt good and warm going down. I'd missed dinner the previous night, so the food tasted extra wonderful. When I finished, I dressed and tried to make myself look somewhat presentable, despite my pale face. Mom looked at me curiously.

"Where are you off to in such a hurry?" she asked.

"I have a meeting," I mumbled as I hurriedly slipped into my old jean jacket. I shivered slightly in the perpetual damp and cold of the tunnels and found myself wishing my jacket was lined.

"A meeting? With who?"

"Capell," I replied, to which mom raised her eyebrows.

"Are you in trouble again?"

"Mom!" I rolled my eyes.

"Well, you do have a track record for being on her bad side."

"I don't know what it's about," I huffed. "She didn't say."

She gave me a hug and cupped my face in her hands. "I'm sorry. I'm just worried about you."

I hugged her again and let her hold me close, like a three year old, and suddenly I felt exhausted. I'd taken care of mom so long, I just wanted a moment for her to take care of me again, like she used to. Tears struggled to force their way out, but I pushed them down again.

"I'll see you at lunch, I guess," I said, avoiding her gentle gaze.

"All right. Keep your nose clean, Lily."

"Yeah, yeah." I grinned.

Mom walked with me through part of the tunnels before she branched off to the kitchens. I headed the opposite direction towards the command center. It was the largest room off of which everything else branched. It had taken so long to get used to the complicated network, but I more or less had a rough idea of where to find the bathrooms, the kitchens, the infirmary and our room.

I settled nervously on a rough wooden bench. Cases came up fairly often that had to be dealt with, so the bench was a sort of place to wait until your name was called.

Wes's face rose suddenly in my mind as I recalled hovering in one of the tunnels off of the command center as he was asked to go back to Epirus to bring allied recruits. My heart thudded painfully, remembering our last, unpleasant goodbye, wanting to beg him to stay with me but not allowing myself to. I wished more than anything he was with me now, holding my hand and keeping me together with his reassuring presence.

"Lily Mitchell," came Capells' sharp, nasal voice. I looked up into her pinched, tired face and rose slowly. The room looked a bit like an amphitheater, with seats on the outer edges and a walled structure in the middle. The walls were really just sheets strung on some PVC pipe, constructed hastily to give some semblance of privacy to each matter that came up.

As I stepped towards the makeshift opening in the curtains, a man came out, shooting a venomous look at me. I stepped back from him, a little shocked. His brows came down low over his eyes, giving him a natural scowl, but I couldn't mistake the look of utter disdain. I'd never seen him before in the tunnels. His bulging muscles strained against a tight tank top, and his hair had been shaved down to the scalp. Between that and the brows, he looked like some kind of thug.

I shivered a little as I stepped into the enclosure and took a seat on a plastic chair facing Capell's desk. She sat with another woman and a man, her number two and three, I supposed. Capell had organized the rebel base into what could be called an anthill, with everybody working responsibly for the whole, but she and the two cronies ran the show. Everyone took orders from them, not seeming to mind, probably because everyone was so desperate for a leader.

"Lily Mitchell," said Capell again, bringing me to attention. I resisted the impulse to salute.

"Yes?" I replied, not knowing what else to say. On reflection, I supposed I should have stayed silent. The man, number three or two, suppressed a smile. I wanted to hug him.

"Green and Briggs and I have been talking about your…abilities. We believe that we have found a mission in which you may be useful to the rebellion."

"Oh." Another lame reply, but what did she expect? A thank you? But even through my irritation, I leaned forward eagerly. Finally, she'd recognized that I had abilities, that I'd been through tremendous things that these tunnel dwellers couldn't imagine in their wildest dreams. Maybe I would even get to work with Wes…

"We have rebel forces within Arduba, itself. Arduba is the capitol city of the south."

"I am aware of the capitol's name, ma'am. I grew up there," I muttered before I could stop myself. She raised an eye, but continued despite her number two's small chuckle.

"This contingent is working on a top secret mission, one that we hope will tremendously turn the tide in our favor."

This time I kept my mouth shut, considering. Ok, not bad. I could be all about top secret missions. And I knew the capitol like the back of my hand.

- 18 -

"This contingent is in desperate need of supplies. You will go with a small group to deliver supplies to the rebel forces within the city. We have organized a rendezvous point at the border. Then you will return here for more instructions."

My mind was racing so fast through getting to play spy that I had to rewind a little. Then it dawned on me. I wasn't going to be working on anything top secret. I'd become the gopher-the gopher of the rebellion.

"I'm...I'm a supply caravan?"

"You and a select few others. You will take orders from Lieutenant Allen. He just left here a few minutes ago."

Now I was taking orders from an ape of a man in a supply caravan?

"That's it, then? I'm a delivery girl?"

My voice had risen dangerously. Capell leaned forward in her seat, looking like a jungle cat ready to pounce on its prey.

"We feel," she said in a steely voice, "that you would be ideal for this mission. Your...abilities could be of help should you meet unsavory people along the way."

"You..." I choked on my rage, barely able to string words together. "You're sending me as a bodyguard? In case we meet other beasts?"

"Well...yes."

That did it.

"After all this time, you're sending me as a delivery girl slash bodyguard, and then you expect me to come running back like an obedient little puppy dog?"

I had stood up without realizing it, my anger getting the better of me. Capell stood up, her hand clutching the gun she had strapped to her hip. For a strange moment, I felt both laughter and shouts rising up inside me, threatening to burst out. Capell was totally *afraid* of me. Actually *terrified* of me. I closed my eyes and took a few deep breaths, trying to let that knowledge be enough. She couldn't do anything to me without her precious gun by her side.

Capell relaxed and let go of the gun. I still felt livid, but at least I also knew now that I had some leverage with this stupid woman. I couldn't believe the ludicrous mission she wanted to send me on, using me for the brawn she so desperately feared.

In a moment, I'd made up my mind. I'd pretend to play along with this stupid little game, then make up my own rules.

"Fine," I muttered. Though I hated agreeing to it, I badly needed to get out of this stinking hole, this prison disguised as a haven. But I would not come back. In my mind, I already began planning what to do. I would get word to mom to meet me and we would leave. We could make our own way, maybe go farther north. Anything had to be better than this joke of a rebellion.

As I stalked away, Capell shouted, "Lieutenant Allen will be in touch with your shortly. Make ready to leave tomorrow morning."

I waved her off and ran, heading for the only spot I knew to go to, the only spot where I could think. I wanted to go outside.

Chapter Four

"Hi mom."

I greeted mom somberly, wishing I didn't have to give her the news. I'd spent the rest of the evening on the cliff, throwing rocks into the turbulent waves and thinking about what to say. Mom was busy all the time and I doubted she'd miss me, but then again, she'd glued herself to my side any time we weren't helping with things around the base.

"Hi honey. I grabbed us some dinner." She offered me a plate with mashed sweet potatoes, noodles with sauce and sliced apples.

"Thanks." I ate ravenously, not realizing until that moment just how hungry I'd been. Before I could escape to the outside, I'd spent the day doing the same menial chores I'd become accustomed to; helping with food preparation, stocking supplies that the trucks brought in, properly disposing of waste in the portable toilets (that was the highlight) and helping welcome new recruits. Not to mention my meeting with Lieutenant Allen. I could tell from the first five seconds of conversation that he held the same ridiculous prejudice as Capell. He'd stated shortly that I was to obey every command issued and that any deviation from protocol could result in capital punishment.

"So?" she asked eagerly, eyeing me. Her food lay untouched. I swallowed uncomfortably, knowing what she wanted to know but stalling for time.

"So what?"

"What did the commander want?"

I scowled, hating to hear everyone call her "commander." She'd never been in one battle that I knew of. She had been in a powerful government position in the north before the split. Her leadership experience was the only thing that got her the title of "commander." For all we knew, she could be a traitor. She'd probably shaken Vic's hand, maybe even had dinner with the guy. I, for one, didn't trust her motives.

"She...gave me a mission."

"Really?" Mom's face registered a complicated mix of worry, pride and surprise. Even she thought I was a renegade.

"Um, yeah. I have to leave tomorrow morning."

Mom's fork clattered to her plate. "Doing what?"

"It's not a big deal. I'm helping deliver some supplies with a group to the border. It'll take a week at most."

"She's sending you to the battle front! No, Lily, you have to refuse it."

"Mom, no one has ever refused the all-powerful Capell. And it's not the battle field. She just wants me there in case we run into some beasts. It shouldn't be anywhere near the fighting."

Oops. Mom went pale, then red. "She's using you as a BODYGUARD?"

"No, mom, I didn't mean it like that. It's more of a liason thing."

"Lily, I cannot let you go. Too much has happened already. If Vic catches you again..."

She shuddered, that hollowed look coming into her eyes. I hated it when she got that look. Anytime Vic or her imprisonment came up, she got this awful face like nothing could ever be good again. It made me feel hopeless looking at it.

"Mom, really, it's fine. You know Capell would never trust me to actually fight. I'm just there for negotiation, IF something happens. She probably thinks it'll be a piece of cake. She doesn't trust me with anything dangerous. Besides, I'll be with the Incredible Hulk, some guy she rustled up for this. He looks like he could kill a bear with a butter knife."

Mom's tense shoulders relaxed a little as a smile crept across her lips. I was the only one who could make her laugh. "Well...I'm going to have a word with the commander just to make absolutely sure it's safe. I don't know if she really understands what you've been through."

I nodded mutely, feeling profoundly grateful that at least my mother could acknowledge that I wasn't some psychotic freak, that I'd been through some really awful things. Everyone else, except the doctor, treated me like I would explode any minute, like a walking land mine, like I couldn't be trusted with anything. I appreciated mom wanting to check things out, but I knew Capell would win. Mom

- 22 -

was the polite, obedient type, never wanting to make waves. Capell would smooth things over, assure mom that I would be in absolutely no danger. Maybe she'd even introduce her to the ape in charge of the group.

Mom bustled off, her food still untouched, to try and talk to Capell. I nestled down in my little bed after throwing my paper plate away, wanting to let my aching body relax. Once again, I found myself thinking of Wes, wondering what he was doing, if he'd been successful in Epirus. The burning pain crept slowly into my heart at the thought of him, his real and total love for me. I knew now that he meant it when he said he needed to fix something there, patch things up with someone, but I couldn't cope with him being away. I wished he were here now, advising me as only he could. Maybe he'd be able to straighten out Capell. Then again, she'd taken an instant shine to him, as if we hadn't been through much of the same things.

My mind clouded over and my eyes grew heavy. I'd just started to drift off when mom rustled her way back into our little room.

"Lily?"

I sat up, rubbing sleep from my eyes.

"I didn't know you were asleep, lay back down."

"No, it's all right, I'm up." I looked at her expectantly, curious to know what Capell said, though I had a pretty good idea already.

"The Commander said you were in good hands," she sighed. "I'm still not one hundred percent about it, but I suppose you'll be safe. You weren't kidding about that guy."

I laughed a little, imagining her reaction to Attila the Hun. "I'll be fine, mom. Who knows, I might be back sooner than you think."

I'd let it slip, not meaning to. Mom cocked her eyebrows curiously, but didn't pry. I was glad. Nobody knew of my plan to leave this wretched place, and I couldn't tell her until the time was right and she'd have to leave in desperation. Most of me felt cocky, confident, but a small part felt a twinge of worry that the old Lily would have felt. Could I really pull it off? Abandon the mission, sneak back into the tunnels and get mom?

We sat up talking a little while about inconsequential things, both of us trying to avoid what tomorrow would bring, but exhaustion finally won. It must have taken mom too, as her soft snores filled our small cave before I'd even drifted off. She'd been hard at work finding ways to make our rationed food go farther, how to grow food in the more cave-like parts of the tunnels, how to make all of it taste better. I reached over in the dark and gently took her hand, feeling again a surge of gratitude that she was still here beside me. I drifted off silently into strange dreams about Wes beckoning me into a swamp filled with writhing snakes.

I woke with a start, not knowing what time it was. Strained voices sounded in the corridor just outside our bedroom, making my heart start to pound faster. I climbed off of my little cot and crept as quietly as I could to our door, straining to hear anything through the heavy metal. Holding my breath, I crouched near the space between the bottom of the door and the linoleum floor, trying to listen.

"I'm afraid it's what we feared, Briggs," came Capell's sharp voice. "The border has been breached. We can't send the supply caravan in to the rendezvous point. They'll have to go straight into the capitol itself, in disguise."

"It's suicide! The supplies can't be that important!" argued a much deeper, growlier voice.

"*These* supplies are vitally important. We all have to make sacrifices for the greater good, and this will have to do."

"These are people we are sending in, including one young girl!"

A pause. "She'll be fine. Don't you know what she's capable of?"

Chapter Five

I sat back against the wall, feeling sick. One quick glance told me mom was still asleep, that she hadn't heard what I had.

So that was it. Capell thought of me as disposable, a human shield for her more worthy minions. I bit my fist, trying to hold back tears of rage, tears of humiliation. After all I'd seen, after all I'd tried to do, fighting fist for fist against Vic to restore some of our lost humanity, this was my repayment, to be served up as a "sacrifice for the greater good."

I looked at mom, guilt wrenching my gut for what I was about to do. I wanted so badly to take her with me, to ensure she'd be safe, but would she ever go along with it? Leave the safety of the base to run away with me, to get as far away from this ugly place as possible?

And what about Wes? Who knew when he'd be back, when or if I'd ever get a letter from him? If I weren't here when he showed up, how would we ever find each other again?

I allowed myself a few minutes of sobbing and feeling sorry for myself. Why did I have to find a disaster at every turn? Why did Capell hate me so much? Hadn't I done quite a lot for the resistance already? She was the self-proclaimed leader of this, after all.

I lay back on my mattress, trying to formulate some kind of plan. Maybe I could kill Capell. I giggled a little, then stopped, feeling shocked over my thoughts. How could I even consider the thought? Sure, the woman was vile, but I could never purposely kill someone.

With a sigh, I rolled over on my side, willing myself to sleep, knowing it wouldn't come. After tossing and turning for an interminable amount of time, I finally sat up and scribbled a quick note to mom, letting her know what I'd done and that I would be back for her as soon as I could. I also added a postscript telling her to destroy the note. I hated leaving her, but I knew she'd be safer here for now where people liked and needed her.

With that, I gathered my bag, the dried heather Wes had given me last summer, some clothes and a few non-perishables and set out. The tunnels were very quiet now, with everyone in their own personal area. I crept quietly through the corridors, squinting against the darkness and relying on the walls to feel my way out. Two months had helped me learn the layout fairly well. When I reached what I thought was the food preparation area, I froze. Voices, quiet and urgent, were floating past somewhere. I could see the beam of a flashlight bobbing in the distance. Looking around frantically, I spotted a supply cart of some kind and jumped between it and the wall.

"Don't know what she expects us to do about it. I mean, if they're coming, they're coming."

"Capell doesn't seem all that concerned about it."

"Why would she? Didn't she used to sit in on meetings with our lovely dictator? I bet she's in on it."

"That'd be a stupid move on her part. One hint that she's a double-crosser and she'd be wiped out."

"I don't know, she's a smooth talker…"

The voices faded, the light bobbed past into another part of the halls. I couldn't help but smirk. I wasn't the only one who didn't like Capell. By the sound of it, some of the others even suspected her. But I didn't have time to worry about or follow up with it now. I had to escape, tonight.

Worry crept through my thoughts as I realized I really didn't have a plan. I had half-baked ideas about trying to contact Wes, but nobody had communicators anymore. I couldn't reach him electronically, and walking from here to Epirus would be suicide. It took four or five hours by train just to make it to the capitol of the north, which meant at least a week walking, if my calculations were correct.

I slid down the wall and settled on the floor, feeling hopeless. Maybe if I went along with this insanity, I could warn the others, let them know what Capell was up to. I might even be able to get word to Wes to come and help me get mom out of here. I knew the north was wild, uninhabited, but maybe we could make a home there. It was worth a shot.

I resigned myself to the fact that it was the only plan I had at the moment. Besides, if I ran off, Capell might come down hard on mom. Shuddering at the thought, I made my way back to our little room and snuggled up on her mattress with her like I used to do when I was a little girl. In time, I fell asleep, my hand clutching tightly to hers.

The next morning, I woke up with mom, who usually woke up much earlier than me. My eyes stung and my head hurt from lack of sleep, but I didn't want to miss any of my last moments with her.

She gave me a long hug as we stood outside the food preparation area where she worked, stroking my hair like she did when I was young. As she pulled back and looked at me, I noticed the shimmer of tears in her eyes.

"Come back safe to me, Lily," she said quietly. "Don't do anything dangerous."

"I'll come back," I mumbled. "Love you, mom."

I wanted to keep things short so I could hold my tears in, but I also wanted to stay with her. So many times we'd been worried that our moments together were our last, what with her sickness and her capture. But I'd never felt that worry press more on me than it did now.

"I love you too." She kissed my forehead, squeezed my hand and met up with her co-workers. We both knew without asking that Capell would not let her see me off.

Feeling an awful sense of heaviness, I dragged myself to the command center and sat nervously on the makeshift bench next to the gorilla.

"If you try anything funny, I'll make you wish you were never born," he muttered.

"Oooh, I'm scared."

A year ago, I would never have said something so bold. Now I just didn't care. Capell filed briskly into the room, cutting off his retort. She had her cronies with her. I wondered which one was Briggs, the man she'd talked to the night before. I pressed my lips in a tight, white line, suppressing the urge to scream at her.

"Change of plans," she barked. "The border has been breached. Capitol troops are patrolling."

She unrolled a huge map of the country and tacked it onto a board behind her. "We've set a route for you through the eastern forest. When the borders were put up, we were not able to extend into the forest due to time constraints. There is an opening where you can enter the southern part of the country. Our men in the

- 27 -

capitol cannot reach the rendezvous point without casting suspicion on themselves. Therefore you will go into the capitol itself."

"But-" Lieutenant Allen let out a gasping choke. "But that's suicide! We'd be spotted for sure! And then captured or killed!"

"These supplies are vital. It is a risk we will have to take."

"How vital can they be? Isn't it just food or something?"

"Lieutenant Allen," Capell thundered, "it is not your business to know what the supplies are. Your only concern is to get them to those who need them."

Allen's face turned bright red, his lips pressed together in a white line, but he sat back down. He knew, probably better than anyone, that you couldn't challenge this woman.

"Is she sending us out on this because of you and all the trouble you make?" he hissed through gritted teeth.

"Probably," I shot back. "If you have an issue, I can show you why she's afraid of me."

He rolled his eyes and lapsed into a moody silence. I slouched in my seat and closed my stinging eyes, wishing that we could just get a move on already.

After some final instructions to Allen, she clamped an awful, metal bracelet around his wrist.

"I like it," I muttered impulsively. "It goes with your eyes."

Allen shot me a sharp look, eyes narrowed. Capell rounded on me. "Glad you like it, Mitchell, because you're next."

"What is it?" I asked, instantly wary.

"A tracker, so we can keep track of your whereabouts and send reinforcements if needed."

"I don't do trackers."

She let out a sharp breath. "You don't have a choice in this matter."

"Slap that thing on me and I'm not going."

She turned on her clackety heel, grabbed a bag lying against the wall and shoved it into my arms. "Fine. You carry the supplies. But don't whine to us if you get injured and we don't know about it."

"Allow me to call the *waaa*mbulance," I said quietly. She didn't hear, but Allen did. And I swear I saw his jaw twitch involuntarily before he carefully arranged his features into a mask of indifference. What do you know, I thought to myself. I'd made the gorilla laugh.

Chapter Six

The wind whipped fiercely against our small vehicle as we drove out across rugged terrain to our drop off point. The sun had just set, making the frosty air even chillier. I'd been outfitted in some kind of Weatherall bodysuit that ran the length of my arms and legs. Thick gloves covered my hands and a strange kind of hood hat covered my hair and wound around to cover my mouth and nose. Every bit of the outfit was black.

Our driver pulled into a remote part of the abandoned town near the tunnels, just behind what looked like an old, dilapidated grocery store.

"Everyone follow my orders. We are a team from here on out, and no one gets left behind," said Allen tersely. We only had two others in the group besides Allen and I, a gangly nerdy guy named Terrence Havermill, and a woman who could best be described as GI Jane. Her name was Amelia Johnson, and she looked roughly in her late thirties or early forties. Tall and very muscular, the scowl on her face betrayed no weakness whatsoever. We'd introduced ourselves after we'd gotten into the vehicle, then sat in stiff silence for the entirety of the twenty minute or so journey. This would be interesting.

Allen climbed out of the car and looked around carefully, then motioned us to follow. He exchanged brief words with the driver before he climbed in the vehicle and took off, stranding us basically in the middle of nowhere. I felt a slight surge of panic, but suppressed it. No way was I going to look weak in front of this lot.

"What about that arm of yours?" said Allen.

I glanced down at my broken limb. I'd completely forgotten about it. Evan had examined me before the mission and was nice enough not to betray his surprise that it was healing so fast. He wrapped it in a more flexible gel cast just to make sure.

"The gel cast will dissolve once my arm is done healing, so it shouldn't be a problem," I replied. Evan explained all about the gel, how it had been engineered and re-engineered for several years in hospitals up north until it had been perfected. It could sense when the bones were once more in proper alignment and then it would dissolve, eliminating another doctor visit. The only flaw in the gel cast was that it could only heal bones after they'd healed for a while. The arm had to heal to a certain extent in a plaster cast, depending on the severity of the break. Then the gel cast took care of the rest, allowing the arm to move without jostling the bones. I'd thought it was incredibly cool, not having ever seen anything like it.

"Whatever. It's your job to keep up," he replied gruffly. "Don't slow down just because of an injury. Capell insisted that you go on this mission, so I don't need you holding us back."

He turned to the others. "According to our instructions, we're to bear east until we reach the edge of the forest. We'll get as far as we can through the forest until daylight, then find a suitable place to camp. Given our vulnerability, we can't travel at all during the day. Everyone clear?"

We nodded mutely, everyone more or less wrapped up in their own thoughts. Allen started off, veering to the left away from the grocery store. Our little group proceeded in a line, Allen in front, Amelia behind him, Terrence third and me last. I liked being behind. It gave me a chance to think without having someone push impatiently from behind.

We reached the trees before long and saw the edge of the half-finished concrete barrier serving as the border. I shuddered a little, thinking how easily enemies could find this gap. As I looked farther down, I saw mottled craters here and there, evidence of earlier bombings. An ill feeling of foreboding cast its shadow over me. Granted, most people stayed out of the woods because of the rumors of the beasts, and the cat was out of the bag on that one. People in the city knew for sure now that the beasts were real, that they'd come out of hiding to take their revenge on the Mainframe. More than ever, people wanted to avoid the woods.

Allen wove expertly through the trees, stopping every now and again to gauge our position with a compass. We couldn't get too far east or we'd be near the coast, well away from our target in the capitol.

After a few monotonous hours of trudging, Allen called for a quick food break. We huddled under some of the thicker trees and ate some dried provisions from the sack that Terrence carried. I ate ravenously, remembering suddenly that it had been ages since I'd had a proper meal. I didn't eat the whole day before we left, my nerves making my stomach jumpy and nauseous.

I felt around the bottom of my plastic sack of provisions and sighed as I came up empty. It would be another few hours before our next meal break, but I'd just have to get through it.

As I put away my plastic snack sack, I felt a small tap on my arm. Terrence stood next to me, a couple pieces of dried fruit lying in his outstretched palm.

"I'm not really a fruit fan. You still hungry?"

I looked up at him and was surprised to see gentle blue eyes sparkling with humor and kindness hidden behind the thick lenses of his glasses. He was thin and wiry, and looked like he could use a good meal himself, but I couldn't refuse such a gesture.

"Thank you," I half whispered as I took the fruit. "Are you sure?"

He nodded, a brief smile touching his lips. Behind the gentleness, I thought I detected a hint of deep sadness, and my heart went out to him. It had been hard the last few months, or years really, to open myself up and trust anyone, but this kindness triggered an instant kinship.

I ate the fruit gratefully, feeling much better than I had when we'd started out. We began our relentless march again a few minutes later. Nobody talked the whole trek, out of fear or nerves, I didn't know. I kept my lips pressed together, trying to keep out the numbing cold. My nose felt like an ice block even with the protection of the Weatherall mask.

At long last, Allen called for a rest as the sky began to lighten. I figured sunrise still had to be at least an hour away, but he probably didn't want to take any chances.

"Fan out and look for a cave or some kind of cover," he said. "Meet back here in ten minutes."

I took the north route, going back the way we came because I didn't think I'd be able to see much anyway. My eyes were so itchy and tired I could barely keep them open.

"I found something," called a deep voice a few minutes later. I turned around and followed Terrence to Amelia, who'd found a sort of small cliff with overhanging moss. The top of the cliff reached over enough that we'd all be able to squeeze into the space underneath and not be seen.

I pulled out my sleeping bag made with the latest heating technology to accommodate temperatures down to ten degrees below zero. I'd heard all about the amazing technology that Capell would send us with when we set out. Maybe she felt guilty sending us out on a suicide mission. Whatever the reason, I wasn't complaining. Climbing into the sleeping bag was like being able to sleep comfortably in a toaster. Within minutes, I'd fallen into a deep, dreamless sleep.

Someone shook me gently. I looked around blearily and saw the sun setting in the west beyond the trees through our little screen of moss. Amelia looked tersely down at me.

"We need to get moving," she said in a surprisingly quiet voice. I'd figured someone like her would bark more than talk, but her deep, reverberating voice sounded strangely calming.

"Okay," I agreed, climbing reluctantly out of my warm little bed. I stretched and yawned, had dinner with the others and packed up all my gear. Within a half hour, we were moving again. The sky grew darker with every step.

"One good thing about winter," gruffed Allen, "is less daylight. More time to travel."

"Oh goody," I muttered to myself. Allen kept talking, seemingly oblivious.

"We're coming up on our first rendezvous point," he continued tensely. "Someone is supposed to meet us there to guide us to the next point. It shouldn't take more than a few hours."

I couldn't be sure if it was my imagination, but I'd seen a slight flicker of apprehension in his eyes. An odd feeling crept up my spine. Something didn't seem right, but I couldn't quite pinpoint it. We trudged along, much as we'd done the previous night. The hours passed a little quicker, perhaps because I felt a little better after all the sleep.

"If my calculations are right, we've hit the coordinates we're supposed to find. Our other soldiers have been informed to meet us in about a few hours. We made good time."

"What do we do until then?" asked Amelia.

"Make camp," he replied. "Mitchell, Havermill, you go gather wood. Johnson, help me set up the tents."

We got to work. Even though Allen made life a little tense with his stern orders, I felt glad for his leadership for the first time. Much of the last few months for me had been spent fearing for my life, running from one horror to the next, never knowing who to trust. A burden had been lifted off my shoulders, letting someone else take the reins for once.

Soon a fire was crackling, the first we'd had since we'd left the base. The warmth felt incredible after the sharp November wind constantly blowing in our faces. Allen finally let us build one, conceding that we'd all be frostbitten if we didn't. Besides, we were deep in the woods now, and the dark could cover the smoke. Hardly anyone ever ventured out here, except extreme hikers, but extreme hiking probably wasn't at the top of people's priority lists right now.

"Here," said Amelia. She handed around some kind of soft bread with tiny little hot dogs.

"Where did you get all this stuff?" said Terrence.

"The kitchens let me have it as a little treat. I've been waiting until we had a fire going. The bread tastes much better toasted."

I'd never been much of a hot dog person, but that meal was the best I'd had since we left base. After we passed around some of our non-perishables, we had ourselves a little feast. My spirits soared higher than they had in a long time. Being away from the confines of the tunnels felt like a breath of fresh air. I gazed up through the clear winter skies, scanning for constellations through the tops of the trees. For the moment, I could forget that our lives were in danger, that we were headed to a war zone. I breathed in the crisp air and relaxed.

"So...what is your story, Mitchell?" asked Terrence suddenly. "I mean, not to be rude or anything. We're just all dying of curiosity, but no one else wants to speak up."

I glanced around at our little crew, suddenly very self-conscious. Everyone stared at me, including Allen. "Um...what do you mean?"

"Well, you just came from the Capitol, on the run from you-know-who, while the rest of us are northerners who've pretty much been preparing for this for years."

"I just...had some trouble. Living in the Capitol and all. Things were getting scary. My mom grew up in the north and she thought we might be safer here."

I liked Terrence and Amelia, but I barely knew these people, and I still hadn't really adjusted to the idea of what I had become. I couldn't tell them that.

"If you mean the rumors from Capell, she's exaggerating a bit," I said hastily, knowing that they wanted to know about my freak power. "I do have some…unusual stamina, but it's just genes. My dad was a weight lifter. My mom was a really good runner. That's all."

I felt a little guilty about how easily the lies came. Everyone seemed to sag a bit, disappointed that I wasn't the freak show everyone expected. Except for Allen. Being in Capell's inner circle had probably allowed him much more access to information about me. Thankfully, he didn't speak up.

Sooner or later everyone laid down to go to sleep. I lay down in my sleeping bag, trying to calm my racing mind, but sleep refused to come. As the fire slowly died into glowing embers, I heard some low throat-clearing sounds. The gruffness sounded a little familiar.

"Is that you, Allen?"

"Oh…uh, yeah. Sorry."

His voice sounded a little strained. "Are you ok?" I asked tentatively.

"Yeah. Just can't sleep."

"Me neither."

I sat up and looked at him from across the fire. In the dying light, I could barely see his face, but I knew he seemed unhappy. He tried to hide it, probably knowing I'd seen his uncertainty.

"What's up with you? Nerves?" he asked gruffly.

He didn't say it unkindly, but I felt a little annoyed at him all the same. Here he was, very obviously nervous, and trying to pin it back on me.

"No. Just wondering what's going to happen next. When our escort will show up."

"Yeah," he replied, more softly this time. "Me too."

We sat in awkward silence for a while, neither of us quite looking at the other. The fire continued to die, the embers withering away one by one into ashes.

"Why did you lie?" he asked suddenly.

So. Capell did have loose lips.

"Well, how would you feel divulging something like that to people you barely know?" I shot back. He paused for a bit. "Besides, whatever you heard was probably exaggerated."

A slight look of fear crossed Allen's face. "She said that you…killed someone. In the Capitol."

A short laugh escaped my lips before I could stop it. "You really believe everything she says?"

The gruffness returned to his face, making it surly. "No. But...you gotta admit, it's a little worrying."

"When Vic was trying to kill *me*, the worst I did was throw him at a fence. Period. Oh, and I accidentally shot a beast in the shoulder, mostly because I didn't know how to handle a gun at the time. It was a pretty insane situation. But he healed. I didn't *ever* kill anyone."

"Oh," Allen replied, avoiding my gaze. I could tell I'd shamed him into silence, but I still felt guilty admitting the things I had done, even though I'd never killed anyone. Those things would haunt me forever. I couldn't be sure I'd ever heal after going through things like that.

"Why does Capell hate me?" I asked suddenly, my voice dripping with bitterness. "What did I ever do to her?"

"I think that she's afraid. Afraid that you'll have more influence than her someday."

That threw me for a loop. I jerked in surprise, feeling the insane urge to laugh again.

"Uh, yeah, don't think so," I chuckled.

"Don't you realize how things changed for us when you came?" he asked, his voice soft, his face serious.

"I didn't change anything. I just came here to get away from everything and everyone chasing me."

"No, Lily," he replied, taking me by surprise. He'd never called me by my first name, or anyone else for that matter. "For the first time, we had real hope. Your mom told everything to Capell, and Capell told it to the inner circle. That's why Johnson and Havermill don't know anything about you. She kept it hushed up so they wouldn't want to get rid of her in favor of someone who actually knew what was going on."

"Whoa, whoa, what do you mean? How could anyone get rid of her? She runs the show."

"Capell has been bumbling a lot of things since she took leadership. She only became leader because she knew about the tunnels. She grew up in that town we went through on the way here, before it was abandoned and she moved somewhere else. I, for one, question where her loyalties lie. That's why, when you came, I knew someone had stood up to the Mainframe and won. Someone made it out alive. Someone with inside knowledge of how the Mainframe works, what their goals and motives are."

"Ok, first of all, if you think I'm so great, why did you get mad when Capell said I had to be on your team for this mission?"

"Well, I thought you'd killed someone. Wouldn't you be nervous having a killer on your team?"

Irritated, I made ready to say no and of course not, then caught myself and laughed. I couldn't blame him.

"Ok, ok, fair enough. But now that you somewhat know me, do you really think I'm a killer? I'm barely eighteen."

"Well, in times like these you never know who to trust." He said it seriously, but a grin flickered across his face.

"All right then, secondly, being barely eighteen, having had this mess come upon me just a few months ago, you should realize that I'm the last person with 'inside knowledge' of the Mainframe."

"You knew Vic's plan though. You knew his plan was to build a super-army. Now at least we know what we're up against. Capell's Mainframe spies all got captured or killed. You are the only one that's been there, that witnessed what's really going on. Capell is mad because she's been made to look weak by a teenager."

The thought hit me like a ton of bricks. Capell, afraid of *me*? In a non-physical way? I wasn't exactly great shakes at being a leader, much less leading a whole revolution. Then again, what Allen said did make sense. I looked at him squarely, realizing for the first time his usually impassive gaze now contained fear, sadness and a tiny glint of hope.

"You know, Allen," I said suddenly, "I don't trust her either. What if we turned this thing over on her head?"

"What do you mean?"

"I mean, go against her little plan. Forget about supplies. I say we gather the remaining spies and troops in the south and just go for it."

"What do you mean?" he asked for a second time, confusion now creeping into the emotions written all over his face.

"I don't know, let's actually fight or something. Forget being her gophers. Maybe we could actually help the people down there make a difference."

Allen looked at me, worry creasing lines into his forehead. "You sure you're not crazy?"

"Promise. Look, nothing is going to turn around in this war unless we take a stand. Will you at least consider it?"

He cocked an eyebrow at me. "You know, I am supposed to be the leader here."

"You are. We can't do it without you. This is just a suggestion."

A small smile curled across his lips. "I'll think about it. If anything, it might be nice to spite Capell." It wasn't a promise, but it was at least a start. He smiled in full now, shaking his head a little. I smiled back, feeling warm despite the chill of the night.

Chapter Seven

Shouts…some kind of odd crackling…heat…*what's happening*?

I opened my eyes slowly, groggily taking in the scene before me. Fire. Lots of fire. Tree limbs crashing to the ground. But why?

The gears in my brain finally clicked into place. Fire. In a forest. I wriggled free of my sleeping back and bolted upright, my arms and shoulders stiff and aching.

"Lily!" I glanced around me and finally saw Allen gesturing frantically to me. I started to pick up my sleeping back, but he waved his arms furiously.

"Leave it! The fire is out of control! We've got to get out of here!"

I took a few stumbling, running steps and managed to hit my stride. Allen joined me as I ran towards him, his hand clutching mine tightly.

"What happened?" I gasped, my words catching in my throat as I breathed the acrid smoke.

"It was a trap," he panted. "They knew somehow we'd be going through this forest. Someone set the fire during the night."

"It's the middle of November!" I shouted hoarsely. "How can a cold, rainy forest burn down?"

"We haven't had any moisture this past year. It's cold, but we haven't had snow or rain. The woods are bone dry."

"Where's Amelia? And Terrence?"

"Scouting ahead." He coughed violently, causing him to stop and double over for a minute. "They're trying to find a lake or somewhere with less trees."

We concentrated on running for a while, dodging low limbs and scrambling through the underbrush. Living in the tunnels hadn't done me much good physically, even though it had only been a few months. I gasped and panted, completely out of track shape, my throat burning as I sucked in each smoky breath.

At long last, we came to some kind of ridge. Allen gave me a boost until I could reach the edge of the ridge. I hauled myself up, then took his hand and helped him. We lay there, at least a mile away from where we'd started, gasping as if we'd never breathed properly before. I sat up and gazed out across the treetops, noticing a patch glowing bright with flames. The fire, luckily, hadn't spread very far, but it would move fast. I'd grown up in the city, but a fire once destroyed one of the major business sections. The squat buildings had gone up like matchsticks. The entire city fire department had to douse it over and over again to get it to stop.

"We need to keep moving," I rasped.

Allen nodded, apparently still too out of breath to talk. "I know. But I thought we could get a little rest and try to see a safer spot to get to."

He stood after a little while. I glanced warily back at the fire, noticing with alarm that the circumference had at least doubled.

"I can see the coast," he reported. "We must have moved further into the forest than we thought.

"I thought Epirus bordered the forest," I replied.

"It does, but we're not that far south yet. This is the upper coast, above Epirus. We'll be safer there."

I looked back at the fire again, growing more nervous by the minute.

"Well, let's get…" I trailed off, noticing something that sent my heart rate spiraling. A lone, straggling figure weaved through the trees, clearly struggling.

"I think I see Amelia!" I cried. "She's at the edge of the flames. We have to get her!"

Allen looked where I pointed. Without a moment's hesitation, he scaled down the edge of the ridge and headed towards her. I scrambled after him, trying to find my footing. Once more I pushed my muscles to the limit following Allen. We caught up to Amelia in a matter of minutes.

"Where's Terrence?" choked Allen, struggling to breathe.

"He's…back….can't get….him up…smoke….too much…" She waved vaguely behind her towards the flames.

"Lily, you get Amelia and head to the coast. I'll go back for Terrence. Hurry!"

"Be careful!" I shouted, feeling a little strange about the amount of concern I felt for him. I shrugged it off and looped Amelia's dirty, smoky arm around my neck. I had to practically drag her towards the ridge. The pace was slow, and my

Weatherall mask was soaked in sweat. I tore it off, aggravated, and gave a mighty heave, struggling to lug Amelia through the smoke.

I skirted the ridge, noting with dismay the sun coming up over the treetops. The coast was safe, but were we being flushed out? Forced out of the cover of the trees to the open where the Mainframe could just pick us up?

I shoved the thoughts from my mind and forced myself to concentrate on getting around the ridge. I thanked my lucky stars I'd seen where Allen pointed the way. I knew I had to get all the way around the circular ridge and keep heading east. Keep heading east. Keep heading east. I repeated the words over and over again in my mind like a mantra.

"How are you doing, Amelia?" I gasped, trying to keep my mind on anything but the fact that I was straining on every level. Even my genetically mutated strength wasn't giving me much. I wondered if my stamina could only last short bouts.

"Okay," she replied wearily.

"Just hang in there, we'll get to the water soon."

Just as I felt ready to collapse, the trees began to thin, the thick forest floor giving way to sand. From deep within me, I pushed for a strength I never knew I possessed. I adjusted Amelia's weight against my shoulder and crawled out onto the sand. The sopping sand felt like heaven against my burned face as I collapsed. We still had some of the shelter of the trees. I didn't dare go all the way out to the water's edge.

"Amelia?"

No response. I struggled to my feet. Amelia lay sprawled on the sand, facedown. My pulse quickened as I stepped over her inert body.

Tentatively, I touched her neck, praying for a pulse. A sigh of relief escaped my lips. She was just exhausted. Some sleep would probably do her good.

I sat back on my heels, my temporary relief evaporated by a new thought. Where were Allen and Terrence?

I glanced warily through the trees, my heart beginning to pound. They should have been right behind us.

I bit my lip, trying to decide what to do. Amelia didn't look good at all, but she had a pulse. She seemed to be breathing evenly. Maybe the shock had worn her out. But what if something worse had happened to her? I needed to stay, but what if Allen needed help?

After going around in circles a few more minutes, I finally took my coat off, draped it over Amelia and plunged back into the forest. Thankfully, the wind seemed to have shifted to a southern direction. The fire hadn't come this way, though I could see it in the distance.

I headed northwest, hoping I'd find the ridge soon. My weary legs screamed at me to stop, but I couldn't leave Allen and Terrence behind. The air grew smoky again, the flames rising up before me like some kind of awful wave. My eyes began to sting.

"Lily!" choked a voice nearby, nearly sending me into spasms. "What are you doing here?"

I turned around and around, looking for Allen, but he was nowhere to be found.

"Down here." I squinted to my right by my feet and saw Allen and Terrence huddled in a ditch.

"What are you doing? The fire is coming!" My voice came out squeaky and hysterical.

"I found a patch with not too much brush, but we'll be surrounded soon. For once I'm glad you can't seem to follow orders. Help me get Terrence. He's unconscious."

I didn't even have time to feel offended by his little comment. I plunged down into the ditch and, using the last of my strength, helped haul Terrence out of the little hole. Both men's faces were red and dripping with perspiration.

I grabbed Terrence's legs while Allen held him under the shoulders. Shuffling through the trees with Terrence was by far worse than struggling through with Amelia. For a skinny guy, he sure was heavier than she'd been. Having to do an awkward squat walk while supporting him didn't help things either. Allen's added strength did help, though, and within ten minutes we'd reached the edge of the sand.

"What are you doing?" I cried as Allen continued out into the open by the water's edge.

"We have to get away from the tree line!"

I turned and noticed with dismay that the flames had again shifted direction. All the foliage near the edge of the sand had become thick with smoke.

As we laid Terrence gently on the sand, I gestured to Allen to follow, too weary to speak. I led him to Amelia, still lying in her spot near the trees, shrouded with my coat. We picked her up and carried her to the sand, laying her next to Terrence.

"Allen…" I tried to say, but exhaustion took over. I collapsed, completely out before my body even hit the ground.

Chapter Eight

"Lily."

A quiet voice broke through the haze in my head.

"Wes?" I groaned, my heart speeding up at the thought of him.

"No."

I opened my eyes, squinting against smoke. Allen hovered over me, looking a little disgruntled.

"Oh, I'm sorry…I thought…" I trailed off, not sure what to say. *I wish you were someone else?*

Allen offered his hand and I took it, sitting up warily. Amelia and Terrence lay nearby. Remembering the fire, I glanced back at the trees. The wind seemed to have shifted again. The trees at the sand's edge were charred, but not enflamed. I could see a bright orange cloud not too far away, with plumes of smoke rising high into the pale sky.

A dull ache began in my head, growing steadily worse.

"Are you all right?" I asked. "What happened?"

"You saved me and Havermill," he replied quietly. "We…we almost didn't make it. I couldn't have gotten him out of that pit, but it was the only place we could have gone. Everywhere else…"

He stopped talking as he glanced back at the trees, clearly lost in his own world. I looked over at the other two again.

"Are they okay?"

He shrugged. "They're breathing. I guess that's all that matters. Let's check them over, though."

We got up and crouched near the others, me with Amelia and Allen with Terrence. I checked all over her arms and legs and any exposed skin for burns or bruises or breaks. She seemed fine, just unconscious, probably from all the shock. Allen said much the same about Terrence, minus a small cut on his hand, probably from a branch. Miraculously, Allen had hung on to his survival pack. He pulled out an antibiotic bandage and gently pressed it to the affected area. My mom had marveled over those bandages for hours, amazed that someone had created a way to imbue the bandage with the medicine so you didn't have to put on medicine beforehand. A random wave of bitterness washed over me, surprising me. I couldn't help it. The Mainframe had been so focused on war, on being the big bad guy that saving lives or other better pursuits had been abandoned. The northerners concentrated on what really mattered; gathering food, improving medicine, *helping* people. That's why they'd become so advanced. If it hadn't been for the discovery of Akrium, maybe the south could have been as medically advanced as the north. Mom might have never gotten cancer. I might have had a father. Who knew?

"You all right, Mitchell?"

"Hmm?" I glanced up at him, confused. "Oh, I'm fine, I guess. Just thinking."

He looked at me, a touch of concern in his eyes. I'd never gotten a good look at his eyes before, with his low brows and all, but what I saw startled me. His eyes were the most amazing color I'd ever seen, a sort of blue-green that shimmered when they hit the light, the color so brilliant they probably could have glowed in the dark.

"What started the fire?" I asked, casting around for a different topic. I felt a little worried by my interest in his eyes. Wes's smiling face came to mind, his boyish features, his mischievous dimple. I tried to focus on that instead.

"I...I don't know, exactly," he said gruffly. "It wasn't the campfire. That was doused thoroughly. I smell trouble, but I can't tell which side it's coming from."

I narrowed my eyes. "What do you mean, which side?"

"I'm...not sure that our location wasn't betrayed. I have a feeling they've got spies on our side. Just like we have spies on their side."

Bile rose in my throat. He couldn't be right, could he? If spies had infiltrated the tunnels, the rebellion was done for. We'd never win. And mom...

"But what if some random soldiers found us? They could have just been jerks, could have set the fire for fun, not knowing what side we were on."

He shook his head. "Something doesn't seem right. I think we were followed. It's odd that our escort never showed up. From everything Capell said,

- 44 -

they should have been there soon after we got there. We traveled fast and came a little early, but not so early that we would have missed them completely."

The thought of Capell made me sick. My mother still lived in those tunnels, working hard and minding her own business. What if Vic knew everything, and just wanted to lull everyone into a false sense of security before he set the place on fire or something?

"We have to go back," I said suddenly, sounding louder than I meant to.

"We can't, Lily. If we have been betrayed, we'll be killed on the spot."

I wanted fiercely to argue that my mother lived there, but I couldn't get past the name thing for some reason.

"Why do you do that?" I asked.

"What?"

"Call me Mitchell sometimes, and call me Lily other times?"

For the first time ever since I'd met him, Allen looked a little uncomfortable.

"Come to think of it, I've never even heard your first name."

"Well, what do you want me to answer first?" That caught me a little off guard. Why did he suddenly care about *my* opinion?

"My first question," I replied.

He shrugged. "I don't know. I usually call everybody by their last name, but talking to you last night made you seem a little more...human."

"Gee, thanks," I muttered.

"I don't mean it that way. I just meant...I had all these crazy ideas about you. I..."

He trailed off, staring glumly down at Terrence.

"You what?"

"Well...talking to you the other night, I just kind of had a weird feeling that I could trust you. That you wouldn't let me down."

"Oh," I replied softly. Suddenly I felt thirteen again, completely self-aware and completely self-conscious. "Um, thanks."

"It's all right," he said, reddening. "Anyway, to answer your second question, my name is...is Levi."

I smiled. "I like it. It's not a name you hear often anymore."

"Yeah. I guess that's why I don't tell people that a lot. They think it's weird."

Suddenly Amelia stirred, followed by Terrence, so the next few minutes were spent assessing injuries and explaining the situation.

"So," said Terrence when we'd made sure no one had been seriously injured, "what do we do now?"

Everyone looked at Allen (er…Levi). He furrowed his brow, then stared at each of them critically, seeming to stall for time. It hit me as I watched his expression. He didn't know if he could trust them, yet he'd told me everything. Surprised, I realized I'd never felt more flattered. I'd been treated like a criminal or a dumb kid for so long that his trust felt wonderfully refreshing.

"We'll continue our course to Arduba," he replied. His eyes flicked towards me once, briefly. I immediately recognized it as a 'we'll talk later' cue. "This fire was an unfortunate deterrent. I can't be sure whether we're being followed, or if our escort got tied up, but we'll make our way."

"But we don't have any supplies," Amelia blurted. "We don't have sleeping bags or anything. We can't survive this cold."

"It will get warmer the further south we go," Allen replied. "And besides, I still have my survival pack if we need medicine." He rifled through the pack quickly, then stood up again. "The woods have a lot of streams for fresh water, but I've only got a few dry provisions in here. We'll have to ration. For everything else, we'll have to rely on our wits."

For a moment, I felt a touch of panic. Amelia was right, after all. I knew Levi was trying to be vague, but it could be dangerous walking out into the forest completely unprotected.

"We're going to have to cut through a lot of wilderness," I supplied. "Does any of us even know the way?"

We looked at each other helplessly. Without even a compass, we could be doomed. Levi squinted up through the trees.

"I can just see the sun through the clouds," said Levi, consulting his watch. "It's not past noon yet, so we're facing east. We need to head southwest, which would be…this way."

He turned and started marching hard through the trees. The rest of us scurried to keep up with him, dodging under low-hanging limbs and clambering over bushes. I wished suddenly that I hadn't ripped off my mask as the bitter chill stung my cheeks.

"Um, Allen, we have a problem," I called, not wanting to reveal his first name to the others.

"What?"

"Aren't we heading into the path of the fire?"

He stopped, glanced around and sniffed the air. A look of uncertainty flitted across his face, disappearing as rapidly as it had come.

"I guess we'll just have to try to outrun it," he replied. "We'll skirt by the eastern shore for a while. When we get far south enough, we'll cut across."

He re-routed and headed south, with us following in a line like ducklings with their mother. The hike lasted all day, without even a midday meal break. Levi chose to ration entire meals rather than just eat smaller meals, thinking that our bodies would metabolize better or something like that. I stared at him as we marched endlessly through the never-ending trees, wondering what was going on inside his head. He had to be worried, wondering if we'd been betrayed. He probably felt a heavy burden too, being the leader, and not knowing if we could even trust each other. In a small way, I felt sorry for him. I felt bad too that I'd initially thought of him as an ape.

Just as the sun began to set, we sat down for a meal, our legs numb, faces frozen.

"It looks like we've cleared the fire, or it's slowed down or something," Levi said tiredly. "I know we should be traveling at night, but we'd probably freeze to death. Better to travel when we have at least some warmth. When we get far enough south, we'll change back to nights."

Everyone nodded, too tired to argue or even say anything at all. "We don't have any blankets," he said. "We'll need to find some kind of shelter and probably huddle together for warmth."

A choked laugh escaped Terrence. "You don't mean share body heat…"

"No, I don't mean that," Levi replied, looking annoyed. "Keep your clothes on, sicko."

That shut Terrence up. He stared down at his hands, a mixture of anger and embarrassment on his face.

By sheer luck, we found a small cave to spend the night in. To minimize awkwardness, Terrence and Levi huddled together, while Amelia and I found a spot on the cave floor slightly smoother than the rest and settled down there. We lay on our backs, arm against arm for warmth.

Exhausted, I quickly fell into a shallow sleep, but awoke some time later to the sound of whispering.

"We're still en route to the capitol," the voice said. "What do you want me to do now?"

I lay rigid, my heart thudding loudly in my chest. I tried to place the voice, but was still a little too sleepy to know for sure. I slowly moved my elbow back, surreptitiously feeling around for Amelia. My arm nudged something soft that suddenly shifted. I heard a small snore escape and knew that Amelia still lay next to me.

"Keep moving towards the capitol," another voice replied, sounding oddly tinny. "The deal is to bring her there. He wants her alive. As soon as she's delivered, we'll re-negotiate with the Mainframe officials. Hurry things along if you can. We can't hold out like this much longer."

It's coming from a communicator. The thought gripped me with terror. Someone had a communicator? Was it Levi? My heart sank at the thought.

Ever so slowly, I lifted my body and turned my head towards the source of the sound. What I saw nearly made me cry.

Terrence sat huddled near the mouth of the cave, his face bathed in the glow of light from the screen of a communicator. I couldn't see the face on the screen, but the clipped tone was unmistakable. Capell. Levi had been right. A traitor stood in our midst, and it was Terrence.

Chapter Nine

I lay back on the floor of the cave, trying to calm my frantic breathing. If Terrence knew I'd heard what he just said...I couldn't even think about it. Terrence! The friendly guy who'd given me extra food. The guy I'd felt instantly bonded to, a traitor! The word rang through my brain like a clanging bell.

What if the food he'd given me had a slow-acting poison in it?

No, Capell had said he'd wanted me alive. He, most likely meaning Vic. I knew it. I *knew* she'd still been friendly with him. After all, she was a politician. She had been the representative for the northern region of Illyria before the war. Negotiation, using people as pawns in her little game, came naturally to her. She'd become the leader of the rebellion, but her way of fixing things was to betray everyone who'd worked so hard for her cause. A hot surge of shame and anger flowed through me, anger at Capell and shame that I'd been stupid enough to fall for it. Sure, Capell was with the rebellion, but her way of dealing with it was offering me up as a ransom, sending me to my sure death like an animal to some kind of primitive slaughter. And I'd taken the bait! To keep the peace and protect mom, I'd taken the bait.

Mom! A fresh wave of horror washed over me as I thought of her, alone in the tunnels, probably being told of my "accidental" death. Mom, who I'd worked so hard to save...

Tears of self-pity and humiliation crept from my eyes, making their silent trails along my cheeks. Terrence had long turned off the communicator and settled back into his spot. When would I ever get a chance to talk to Levi alone? I couldn't trust Amelia. Perhaps she was in on it too. In some inexplicable way, I knew I could trust Levi, despite everything he'd thought of me before. He wanted freedom. I could see it in his eyes.

Somehow, I drifted into an uneasy sleep, but it didn't last long. I woke with a jerk at one point, feeling a stinging pain in my neck, but nothing moved or made a sound in the silent night. I figured it for a pinched nerve and tried to sleep again, but only caught a few winks.

My eyes felt coated in sandpaper when they next opened, groggily taking in everything around me. The cave, with pre-dawn light filtering in through the opening, was filled with the others still lying asleep in their makeshift beds. The sight of Terrence, lying sprawled on the cave floor with his mouth hanging open, made me sick.

Traitor.

The word kept ringing through my mind, my anger flaring each time I looked at him. And yet, I suddenly realized, he wouldn't be considered a traitor. When this was all over, he would be looked at as a hero, the one who turned in the freak that started this whole mess and restored peace to Illyria.

Some peace, I thought bitterly. Why couldn't any of them see how dangerous Vic really was? Now that he had the secret of the cure, it would take him no time to build the army he'd always dreamed of, take over Illyria completely, make his way down to Epirus and then what? There'd be no stopping him.

I jumped as someone grunted and rolled over. My heart calmed slightly as I saw Levi stir and sit up. He blinked at me groggily, then looked at his watch.

"What're you doing up?" he asked blankly.

A sudden urgency took over, making my heart pound again. "Can you walk with me to get some wood for a fire?" I asked, praying that for once he wouldn't bellyache about people seeing the smoke during the day.

"We can't," he replied with a large yawn. "You know someone would see the smoke."

"We really need to get some wood." I tried to carefully exaggerate each word. "It's freezing cold in here."

I gave a pointed look at the others and suddenly he got it. "Yeah, all right, I guess just this once."

He shrugged himself out from under his heavy coat, which he'd been using as a blanket, and put it on. We hustled out of the cave, not speaking until we'd gone a good dozen yards or so away.

"What's really going on?" he asked, stopping suddenly once we were far enough away from the cave.

"I woke up last night. Terrence was on a communicator. Talking to *Capell.*"

He stared at me, nonplussed. "Yeah. She gave us a communicator to keep in touch. They use an un-broadcasted channel."

I took a step back, unexpectedly wary. "Ok, then," I replied slowly, "but do you know what they were talking about?"

"Something about the mission, I'm sure. She was probably asking about our progress to Arduba."

I felt my heart sink. Was he in on it too? I brushed hair from my eyes and looked up at him. I immediately regretted it. His incredible eyes shone softly in the early sun, making him look suddenly younger, less stressed, more…handsome.

No, I said, shaking myself. *He may be a traitor, too.* I couldn't help but notice, though, that the thought of him as a traitor weighed on me heavily.

"Yes, it was about the mission," I said carefully, "but do you know exactly *what* the supplies are?"

He frowned, confused. "Yes. Provisions and medical supplies. That's why I hung on to the survival pack. We were to meet…"

"No, you idiot! I'm the delivery! I'm the cargo!" I shouted, my frustration getting the better of me. "Why do you think the route suddenly changed? Why do you think the escort never met us? They're delivering *me* to the capitol, using me as a negotiation tool with Vic! The supply run was a distraction to keep everyone from suspecting! Terrence is here to make sure the *real* job gets done!"

His mouth opened and closed a few times in shock. He leaned against a tree, gathering his thoughts.

"Are you positive about this?" He looked a little ill.

"Why would I make this up?"

He sat down, right there on the forest floor. "I don't know," he replied, cradling his head in his hands. "I don't know what to believe anymore."

"Believe me," I whispered, crouching down to be eye level with him. "You said you can trust me. I feel like I can trust you. We can turn this thing over on her head. Do some real fighting. Win this dumb war."

He looked up. "As noble as that all is, Lily, we can't just march in there, banners blazing. We'll do nothing but get ourselves killed. Besides, we have to deal with the problem of Terrence first."

I sat down in the damp leaves. "What about Amelia? Do you suspect her?"

"She was called in at the last minute," he replied. "She's gruff and all, but I don't think she's in league with him. Terrence has always been pretty near the top of the hierarchy in the rebellion. Capell usually just uses me for my brawn. Amelia's a lot like me, a lieutenant, being pulled into certain tasks because of her strength."

"Well, can we get rid of him? Give him the slip?"

He frowned again, his face laced with disgust. "I don't know. Maybe. It would take planning, though. I can't believe we saved that good for nothing scumbag, then he turned around and kept right on with his plans."

"Maybe he's under orders, with threat of death."

Levi cracked up. "*What*?"

"Seriously!" I cried, annoyed that he could even think of laughing at a time like this. "I wouldn't put it past Capell."

He shook his head, a gentle smile on his face. "I'm sure he's more motivated by the honors Capell could give him once the war is over. He'd probably be set up for life, too. She wouldn't hold a death threat over one of her top Sergeants."

"Well, whatever," I grumbled, more than a little frustrated at not being taken seriously.

"What have you gone through that's made you so cynical?" he asked quietly. His face had softened, his features lined with a gruff kind of sympathy. I stared back at him, unsure of what to say. If he'd only known everything I'd been through, he'd definitely have an idea why I'd suddenly become so paranoid. A chord of longing struck within me as I remembered Wes, the one who *did* know everything I'd been through. I missed him so badly I could hardly keep tears from choking my response.

"You wouldn't want to know." I stood up and looked at the sun streaming through the trees. "We should get going. Terrence might get suspicious. And we'd better gather some wood too so we have some excuse for being out."

I gathered up some dead limbs and twigs, remembering to look for dry wood. Avery had taught me so many things in the brief time we'd traveled together. I wished she were here now, helping us, being the decisive leader that she always was. Especially now that things had gone way south with the mission.

Levi followed me without a word, mimicking my actions of picking up dry wood from the forest floor. After twenty minutes, we had a pretty good stack. It didn't take long to get back to the cave. Amelia and Terrence were already up, rooting around for some breakfast.

"Where did you two go?" asked Terrence, eyeing us carefully. "Oh, never mind."

He had seen the wood and been fooled. I breathed a silent sigh of relief.

"We'll stay here another day, get our strength back," said Levi. "We had a pretty rough time of it outrunning that fire. In the meantime, we will try to make some more supplies since we lost quite a bit in the fire."

The day passed tensely as Levi and I shot one another furtive looks. Terrence talked and laughed like his usual self, but I noticed a steely glint in his eyes I hadn't seen there before. What I'd taken for friendship had really been keen interest, taking in each thing we said to know how to use it against us. I realized I was probably being a bit paranoid, but you could never be too careful.

When night fell at last, we built a fire since the night sky would hopefully hide the smoke. We ate a bit of our meager provisions and even a few small fish that Terrence and Levi had caught from a nearby stream.

Later in the evening, I sat trying to weave a sort of basket backpack out of springy pine needles and getting nowhere fast, when Levi came in from scouting. Terrence was still presumably out, leaving just him, me and Amelia. He brushed past me, and something white fell into my hands. A note scrawled hastily on a small scrap of paper.

After the others are asleep, leave the cave and walk fifty paces straight from the mouth. I'll meet you there. Not a word to the others.

I frowned, weirded out by the cryptic instructions, but tucked the paper furtively into the pocket of my coat. Maybe Levi had a plan, any kind of plan to get out of this mess. Since I was out of ideas, I had no choice but to follow instructions.

Chapter Ten

A few hours later, I crept out of the cave after I'd seen Levi go. The others were definitely asleep, passed out on the floor, wrapped up in their coats. I shrugged into my own coat and crept as quietly as I could out into the forest.

There he was, waiting among a thick cluster of trees, just as he'd said he would. He turned at the sound of my footsteps.

"You're like a train running through here," he said with a grin. "Anything fifty miles away would hear you coming."

"Why the need for stealth?" I shot back. "I'm pretty sure there's not another soul for miles around anyway."

He raised his eyebrows warningly. "Don't forget, there's a traitor around."

I shrugged. "Okay, okay. So what's this all about? I feel like I'm in some kind of crazy mystery or something. Why so cryptic?"

"We don't know who to trust just yet. I figured the more vague the note, the better."

I folded my arms, trying to shut out the cold. "Fair enough. What are you thinking, then? What do you want to do about Terrence?"

He let out a deep breath. "I'm still not entirely sure. I figure we should alert Amelia, but I don't know how with Terrence hanging around. I thought about having him scout tonight when we get back and then explaining the whole thing to her. We're stretched for time as it is. Terrence is anxious to leave."

"Yes, I am," said a deep voice behind us. An icy feeling of terror gripped my heart as I turned around. There stood Terrence, a gun in his hand.

"You two are so predictable," he sneered, stalking towards us like a cat towards its prey. He held up his hand, a small white paper clutched between the thin fingers.

"Lily!"

I turned to look at Levi, my throat turning dry. I must have dropped the note somewhere in the cave! How could I have been so stupid?

I swallowed the lump in my throat and backed up slowly, weighing my chances. If I ran, it was pretty much fifty fifty that I'd get shot. Not to mention Levi.

"We know what you're after, and it's out of the question. If I'd known what this was all about, I never would have agreed to it," spat Levi.

"Now, now, surely you're the agreeable type, Lieutenant Allen," Terrence hissed. "The girl is dangerous. She's caused the upheaval of the whole government. Commander Capell is right to turn her in. The bombs will stop falling, both sides will call a truce. It'll all be over if you'll just help, Allen."

I looked over at Levi, sick at heart. The offer did sound appealing. Would he really sell me out like that? Levi's eyes narrowed further. "You'd turn in an innocent girl just to save your own hide, Havermill? That's pretty low, even for you."

My heart leapt a little despite the terror of the situation. Levi looked at me once, briefly, and I knew without a doubt he would never turn me over.

Terrence made a face. "She's not so innocent, as you well know."

"You really believe all that crap Capell spouted? You really think she's capable of murder? She's only eighteen!"

"Desperate times make people do crazy things. I wouldn't trust the little viper as far as I could throw her." Terrence cocked the gun. "Don't make me do this the hard way, Allen." His finger reached for the trigger…

"Stop!" I cried. My heart hammered in my chest, unable to handle the horrible visions of a lifeless Levi slumped on the ground, a bullet wound in his chest. Terrence would shoot. I had a gut feeling he'd shot someone before, maybe even a few people. He was a maniac. His bulging eyes made that much clear.

"I'll go, okay? Just don't hurt him," I choked.

"Lily, no," Levi grunted, his teeth gritted. "If this fool wants to-"

"I'm *not* going to let him shoot you," I replied. I turned to Terrence. "But if I come, Levi comes as well, with no consequences. This doesn't come back on him, do you understand me? You make sure of it when I'm…I'm gone."

"Lily, no!"

Levi looked positively livid now, his fists clenched up, his face white.

I looked at him sadly, feeling horrible that it had come to this. I really had no guarantee that he would be protected, but what else could I do? I'd bargained myself before.

"I don't want to see you hurt."

Levi seemed a little taken aback for a moment. He stared at me, seeming lost for words, his eyes searching mine.

Terrence smirked a little as his finger relaxed away from the trigger.

"Fine with me," he muttered. "Nobody cares about him. It's you we need."

Terrence turned around and walked behind us, herding us back in the direction of the cave, his gun still out and ready in case we decided to run. Levi's face remained taut with rage. I reached out and gently grabbed his hand.

"It's not true what he said, by the way," I whispered, not wanting the traitor to hear.

"What do you mean?" he asked.

"About nobody caring about you." I stopped, the words suddenly stuck in my throat, feeling crippled by my own bashfulness.

"You don't have to feel sorry for me," he replied. "I'm not obsessed with moving rank like our little friend back there."

"I don't mean it that way," I rambled. "I just mean…I mean, I care about you. As a person. As a…a friend."

The fear and anger melted from Levi's face as he looked at me. A soft, inexplicable sort of look gathered in his eyes. "I care about you too, Lily."

We reached the cave and Terrence made us gather up our supplies. He wanted me in a coat since Vic wanted me alive.

"Where's Amelia?" he grunted.

For a moment, fear gripped my heart again as I wondered if she'd known all along. Then again, if Terrence was the traitor and didn't know where she was, perhaps she wasn't on his side after all. A tiny flame of hope erupted within me. Maybe she'd put two and two together and had gotten out for help. I said a silent prayer for her well-being, that she would somehow make it back to the tunnels and be safe. I wished more than ever that I'd had time to ask her to take care of mom for me. We hadn't talked much, but she'd seemed kind, in a gruff sort of way.

"Blast her! We don't have time to wait. She can starve in the woods or be eaten for all I care," he muttered, making me hate him even more. "Move out."

Hours later, we trudged on southward through the woods. There would be no sleep that night. Levi continued to hold my hand, and I let him, though I felt a slight twinge of guilt as I thought about Wes. I couldn't dwell on it too much, however. More gruesome thoughts occupied my mind, wondering what fresh horrors awaited me in the capitol.

"Let's break," Terrence said suddenly from the back of our little caravan. "Not too long, though."

We sat down on a couple fallen logs, bone weary and about to collapse. Terrence sat farther away from us, eating the rest of our provisions right in front of us. He was probably doing it to intimidate or weaken us. So much for getting us there alive. A feeling of intense hatred stole over me as I watched him stuff his face. He was no better than Capell or even Vic.

"Sorry I don't have any extras this time," he jeered, winking at me. I stuck my tongue out at him. It wasn't mature, but it felt good to do it. Levi stifled a laugh next to me.

Levi. Though I had much bigger problems to deal with, I felt increasingly more worried about what was happening between he and I. I couldn't deny the fact that I felt really attracted to him. His strong, quiet assurance was the only thing holding me together at that point.

"I'm sorry about all this," he whispered as Terrence continued to eat. "I didn't mean for any of this to happen."

"It's not your fault," I reassured him. "I should have known there wasn't anywhere safe. It's probably better this way. I'm a danger to everyone I meet."

He stared at me intently, his eyes sympathetic. "You can't help everything that's happened to you."

He put his arm around my shoulders, revving up my heart rate. Half of me wanted to lay my head on his shoulder, cuddle into him as close as possible, but the other half of me panicked. I didn't really know for sure what had happened between Wes and I before he left, but I still felt like I belonged with him. Levi was missing some of my favorite qualities that were abundant in Wes. I missed Wes's sense of humor, the fact that he could keep my heart light despite all the problems. Wes knew everything about me. Levi didn't. For that matter, I barely knew Levi. And yet...Levi made me feel like I'd never be threatened again, as if all he cared about were protecting me. Wes's sudden departure still stung.

Without realizing it, I'd closed my eyes and begun to drift off, my head drooping forward onto my chest. I looked up at his face, dim in the light of the stars. He took his hand and gently tilted my head onto his shoulder. Tired and scared, I didn't argue. I wrapped my arm around his waist and let his warmth envelope me.

Chapter Eleven

"Get up!"

I jerked awake from my position on Levi's shoulder. Terrence stood, hands on hips, glaring down at us. Levi took my arm and helped me up, as Terrence took up his position behind us. I walked shakily for a while, still half asleep, as Levi supported me by the arm.

After a few more hours of trudging, the sky began to lighten. Rain also began to fall, making my heart sink. Already weary and ready to drop, the path became more and more slippery as the rain poured down. Terrence never let up, keeping us at an even pace the entire time. He seemed more machine than man, able to walk insane distances without having to stop. He did have the advantage of having eaten all our food, though.

The trees steadily began to thin, and the rain became slightly warmer. We'd covered a lot of distance. After a while, I didn't even need my coat. Levi had taken his off long ago. Every now and again, he smiled back at me encouragingly. I found it hard to believe that this was the man who'd once been wary and suspicious of me.

"Let's stop here," Terrence grunted. "No falling asleep this time."

Terrence slumped gruffly onto a fallen log. With nowhere else to sit, I parked on the carpet of wet leaves, not caring about the moisture since I was already soaked. An uncomfortable tightness had settled in my nose. A cold was coming. Probably all the exposure and exhaustion. I rubbed my eyes wearily, trying not to think about what lay ahead.

"You okay?"

I looked up to see that Levi had settled next to me. "Yeah. Tired. You okay?"

He shrugged. "I've been trying to figure something out," he said, lowering his voice conspiratorially. "Something to get us out of this mess. I haven't given up."

Despite my exhaustion and pain, a slow warmth coursed through my heart at his words. It felt good to at least know I wasn't alone.

Terrence seemed to be thinking hard, staring down at his combat boots and rubbing his chin. He probably had a plan working in his mind as well, a plan for how to get me to Vic in the quickest possible way. Normally, I would have felt hatred at such a moment, but my overwhelming fatigue helped me not care. Maybe people would be happier when I was gone. The war might end. Then again, with all the lies Vic was always pumping out, maybe not. I laid my head wearily in my hands, feeling that nothing mattered anymore.

Levi suddenly laced his fingers through mine and squeezed tightly. "Don't give up."

His earnest gaze pierced me in some strange way that I couldn't quite fathom. He really meant it. They weren't just empty words. The flame of hope sprang up in me once again, and some of my weariness ebbed away.

Much of the day was spent marching endlessly, slowly towards the end goal. The terrain became tricky at points, requiring us to slog up hills, through tight canyons and over rough, bumpy ground riddled with upraised tree roots.

As day wore into night, my stomach screamed with pain. This time of year, not even berries or nuts grew. Levi and I had no chance to even secretly forage. Terrence had clearly underestimated the length of time it would take to reach the city. He'd eaten every last dry good in the survival pack, making his mood go from unpleasant to downright foul. He started spouting words I'd never even heard, complaining about everything from the forest animals to his shoes.

"Let's break," he muttered angrily as the first stars began to wink into existence in the sky. It was the third break we'd had that day. He checked the gun to make sure it was loaded, making my heart race. I imagined Levi and I in a large pot, simmering while Terrence sprinkled us with seasonings. It was ridiculous, of course, but I didn't know what to think at that point.

"You two gather firewood and start a fire," he groused, throwing a small book of matches at us. "I'm gonna kill one of those squirrels and eat it if it kills me."

He didn't get far when he suddenly crumpled, howling in pain and clutching his leg. He tried in vain to stand, but crumpled again as something hit his other leg.

"Don't attempt to get up again," said an icy voice, "or I will shoot."

I stared at Levi, my mouth gaping open ridiculously. Like some weird apparition, a slim, tall man stepped out from between the trees and approached us. He looked odd, dressed in some kind of odd bodysuit with a hood. A long, slender, wooden bow lay clutched in his white hand. A quiver of arrows was slung neatly around his waist.

"So you're the one all the fuss is about," he said, eyeing me.

"Who are *you*?" I knew I sounded rude, especially to someone who'd just shot the bane of my existence, but constant fear and paranoia can do that to a person. He gave a tight-lipped smile.

"Name's Eli," he said, extending a hand. "A friend of yours got word to me that you were in trouble. I'm a well-known tracker, but I didn't really have to rely on my skills the way you guys were crashing around like that."

He jerked his head towards Terrence. "Need me to finish him off?"

I gaped at him. He said it as casually as if he'd asked us if we wanted some gum. I didn't particularly love Terrence or anything, but it seemed cruel. I looked over to see him lying on the ground, blood pouring profusely from both calves where the arrows had stuck. He'd removed them, but the wounds were deep. His eyes opened wide with terror as he mouthed the word "no" over and over again.

"That won't be necessary," said Levi, giving Terrence a look of disdain. "Is there anywhere he can be held?"

"We have a rebel camp not too far from here. You guys up with the contingency in the north? The ones calling themselves the 'leaders?'"

"We'd prefer not to say," said Levi carefully.

Eli just laughed, then gave a loud whistle. Behind him came a stocky figure with hair down to her shoulders. She smiled grimly and shrugged as she stepped closer.

"Amelia?" I gasped.

"Looks like we got here just in time," she replied.

"Think you can trust me now?" Eli said with a smirk.

My head spun. Without thinking consciously about it, I grabbed Levi's arm for support.

"Tell you what," Eli said, his voice slightly less stiff. "Let's find a cave or something and eat. You guys look half starved."

I followed obligingly, my attention caught at the word "eat." A few more random people melted out of the trees and slung Terrence between them in some kind of makeshift stretcher. Amelia sidled up next to us.

"I smelled trouble when I saw Terrence leave the cave. I could tell something was up, especially with the way you guys were acting. I didn't know who to trust, but caught a few glimpses of him carting you two off and figured it out pretty quick."

"How…"

I couldn't finish my sentence. My tongue refused to work under all the extreme conditions of cold, exhaustion, hunger and confusion.

She smiled. "These guys are what you'd call vigilantes. They're part of the rebellion, but didn't want to join with the northern faction. They're fighting guerilla style down here in the south."

"How did you know about them?" Levi asked.

"I make it my business to know the ins and outs of every cause I pledge myself to. Capell is a total idiot, but I wanted out of the north faction, so I jumped at this mission. I'm from the south and I'd seen just how bad it was before I moved north for work a few years ago. I didn't know that Lily was the cargo, but it's disgusting. Terrence will be taken care of."

"You're not going to…you know…" I trailed off, not wanting to think about the gruesomeness of it all.

"No, though he does kind of deserve it," she muttered. "He'll be put into a prison of sorts. Traitors to the rebellion are far worse than the opposition."

I smiled gratefully, not knowing what else to say. I felt bad for previously thinking that she looked like a man. She'd saved our lives.

We found a small overhang under a cliff where we could rest for the night. Terrence's wounds had been treated and his wrists bound. The stretcher lay beside him. He still had to be carried. He sat sullenly on the ground near the fire, his dark, shadowed face a stark contrast to the cheerful flames. The trackers gave us some really good food, most likely stolen; soft, wheat bread, clear, cold water, dried strawberries, some dried, salted pork and potato chips. The meal, though mostly made of food storage, tasted like heaven. I ate my fill since they had more than enough for all of us, and settled back against the rough wall of the overhanging ridge. Levi settled next to me.

"So what exactly do you guys do?" I asked, my exhaustion somewhat alleviated with the food. I could actually talk now without getting tongue-tied.

Eli swallowed and shrugged. "Keep an eye out for troublemakers."

He gave half a smirk that disappeared almost instantly. I had a feeling he was being shifty on purpose, maybe because he'd actually killed people, or maybe because he just didn't like to talk about what he did. Maybe he was trying to enjoy the small break, like me. For whatever reason, I didn't push it. I figured he'd talk if he wanted to.

"Are you okay?" asked Levi. "I feel stupid for not getting us out of our situation, but I guess it was good luck that Amelia came."

His hand twitched slightly, making me feel weird. I wondered briefly if he wanted to hold my hand.

"I'm fine, thanks. Don't worry. You don't have to be the hero all the time."

"I wanted to be," he mumbled, looking shyly down at his lap. "I hated seeing you in trouble."

A flush rose in my cheeks. *Stop it!* I commanded myself. No matter what happened here or how far away Wes was, I couldn't betray him. My heart ached at the thought, as much as the pain of him leaving.

"Well," I replied briskly, "we're all right now. We've just got to figure out our next steps, I guess."

"Yeah," he said vaguely, clearly uncomfortable. "Best thing to do is get some sleep."

He moved closer to the fire and curled up under his coat. One of the trackers offered me an extra blanket. I took it gratefully and lay down, trying to ease the stiffness from my limbs. Every muscle in my body ached, and my throat was quickly becoming scratchy. It took a long time for sleep to come.

Chapter Twelve

The next day dawned gray and cold, without even a hint of sunshine peeking through the iron clouds. I stretched, my muscles even more cramped now from curling under the blanket all night. As I sat up, I noticed most everybody was already awake, including Levi. He stood with Eli, deep in conversation. He turned and noticed I was awake, so he quickly wrapped things up. His face seemed brighter, more full of color than previously.

"So what are we doing?" I asked as I rolled my shoulders to crack my sore back.

"Eli says the best thing to do is get him to one of their safeholds," he replied, jerking his head towards Terrence. Terrence hadn't woken up yet. He lay curled against the overhanging ridge, looking uncomfortable in his bounds. For a moment, I felt a slight bit of pity for him. After all, he'd never bound us, even at night. Then again, he had threatened us with a gun. It suddenly occurred to me just how awful this war had become. Even those who fought for freedom treated prisoners horribly, showing no mercy. Some could argue it was deserved, but was it really?

"When do we leave?" I asked, trying to shake off my uneasy thoughts.

"As soon as we clean up camp," he replied. "It's not too far from here, about a day's march."

We gathered our things and secured them in packs. One of the trackers rudely woke Terrence with a kick to the ribs and a command to get up. He stood as best he could with arms bound behind his back, scowling at his captors. Eli slung his bow neatly over his shoulder and took the lead.

We walked in a much larger caravan now, the six trackers scattered throughout the line, Terrence in the lead, Levi and I in the middle and Amelia bringing up the rear, making our party ten. No one said much, everyone still recovering from the previous day. Terrence could now manage a stiff, jerky gait, but he still didn't walk incredibly well. Who could blame him? He'd nearly been crippled the day before. I was surprised he could walk at all at this poing. As cruel as I felt they'd been to him, they had bandaged his legs tightly and well. They'd also given him food to eat and water to drink. My head swam with the confusion of it all. A worse punishment, in my opinion, would be to send him back to the rebel base with his tail between his legs, admitting defeat. Then again, who knew what he would do? It might give him the opportunity he needed to turn us all in. I wondered briefly if he started the fire.

"We're nearly there," announced Eli presently. "Let's break for a midday meal, then it should be only about two or so hours."

We sat down and ate some more of the fare from the previous night. The chips and bread were a little stale, but tasted good all the same.

A small sound reached my ears, growing louder all the time. Crashing brush, twigs snapping...someone was hurrying quickly through the woods.

"Do you hear that?" asked Levi, his voice tight with tension. I nodded and signaled him to be quiet. Eli had heard it as well, judging by the look on his face. His eyes scoured our little clearing frantically.

"Put the food away," Eli commanded, his voice low and hoarse. He looked around again, his teeth gritted. He pointed suddenly to a small hill overgrown with tangled underbrush.

"Everybody move. Stay low, under the brush. Quick!"

We rushed to the hill and crawled into the brush, which, to my dismay, was covered in thorns. I scooted on my belly under a particularly gnarly bush. Levi lay under a wild shrub to my right, and Eli ahead of me at the top of the hill, looking down. The others had found various places behind us.

Before long, harsh voices could be heard. I scooted closer to the edge of the hill and moved so I could get a view of our clearing. Eli softly cursed, and suddenly I knew why. Footprints. Everywhere. We hadn't taken the time to clear them off.

Too late. A couple of huge, burly men suddenly emerged, their heads shaven, their massive biceps bulging from t-shirts with the sleeves torn off. It had to be thirty or forty degrees out, but they didn't shiver in the slightest. Their eyes flashed eerily in the sunlight, making my heart stop. They were beasts, but not the sickly, pale people I'd seen in the forest a few months ago. These men looked healthy, robust, completely…normal. The akrium seemed to have no effect whatsoever on them.

I gasped. Eli shot me a dirty look, but I didn't care. I thought back to that day when Wes and I infiltrated the beasts' lair, the man who'd hated me so much for being healthy when he wasn't. He'd had access to the cure. He'd been there the day we fought Vic. As the horrible truth dawned on me, I wanted to cry.

"Will you stop crashing around?" hissed one beast, looking at his companion.

"We're not on a path, so how can I *not* crash around?" the other shot back. "There's nobody out here. Lycus is batty."

"He told us to look everywhere, dimwit. This just happens to be where we're stuck looking."

Lycus! I remembered with a jolt to my heart that Lycus had been that beast's name, the one who'd hated me. I'd been hoping I was wrong, that my theory was totally off base, but here before me was the proof. I buried my face in my arms, trying to flatten myself into the ground. If they found me, there was no telling what would happen. Lycus and a few other beasts had just disappeared without getting on the train to the north. Most people assumed they'd just missed it, or decided to go back to the forest, but never knowing had made me very uneasy for the last few months.

"Wait," said the one who'd spoken first. "Look! Footprints! Someone's been here recently."

There went the hope that they'd be too dumb to look down. Then again, if they were bounty hunters, they'd obviously be looking for footprints. Duh.

I swallowed hard as I listened to them shuffling around the clearing. Every now and again, the one I assumed to be the leader shot commands at the other to step around the footprints, to look carefully for anything that might give a clue to who'd been there. The other one grumbled and groused. I raised my head slightly and looked at them again, hoping against hope they didn't find a clear trail leading up the hill where we hid.

"OW!" howled the complainer, suddenly clutching his arm. He looked around his feet and bent down, standing up with a sleek metal arrow in his hands. "What the…"

I looked up the hill to see that Eli had managed to crouch down and fire his arrow without so much as a leaf rustling. I wanted to scream at him that he'd give our position away when he fired another. This one whizzed towards the leader, who clutched his leg a moment later in pain. They whirled and looked for Eli, but couldn't seem to see him. I realized Eli was aiming not to hit, but to graze. He was some marksman, but would soon get us killed the way he was carrying on. They'd figure out sooner or later where the arrows had come from.

Another arrow caught the dumb one on the hip. "Somethin' ain't right with this place!" he hollered. Before the other could stop him, he ran off into the trees. The leader had no choice but to follow him.

I felt really stupid all of a sudden. Eli wasn't just showing off. I realized now that he'd aimed the arrows so they wouldn't cripple the men, just scare them off. It had worked, but he didn't know that those men were imbued with the power of cured akrium, that those surface wounds would take mere hours to heal. By then, the leader would convince the complainer that they needed to get back to the clearing and look again at the footprints.

After several tense minutes, Eli wriggled free from the thorny bush where he hid, his pale skin now covered with angry red scratches.

"Get up," he commanded, his voice rough. "We've got to leave. *Now.*"

Chapter Thirteen

Eli, as the unspoken leader, hurried us down the hill and in the opposite direction the beasts had fled. Ignoring Levi's confusion, I shoved my way through the group of other trackers towards Eli.

"What in the heck are you playing at?" I hissed as I trotted up next to him. His long, willowy legs covered much more distance than my short, stubby ones, making me have to jog just to keep up. He stopped abruptly, catching me mid-stride and making me do a strange looking stop and twirl move.

"What do you take me for, an idiot? Yes, I know what they are. Don't scold me, little girl, when you have no idea what you're talking about."

Little girl?? My hackles went up as I stared him down. "They're beasts," I shot back, earning a small smirk from Eli. I hurried on, "People injected with akrium. But you're missing the bigger point here."

He rolled his eyes. "And what would that be?"

"They're *cured*," I said slowly, as if he were deaf. "They have all the advantages of akrium without the poisoning."

He raised his eyebrows skeptically. "How on earth would you know something like that?" he challenged. "And besides, everyone knows that no cure exists."

"Back in the summer, I found the base camp of the bea- the original people who'd been injected, the scientists. My dad was one of them, but he died from the poisoning. I was born after he'd already been injected. I have the powers of the akrium, without the side effects. With my DNA, those scientists created a cure. That's why everyone has made such a fuss over me, as you so eloquently put it."

For the first time, Eli looked appropriately taken aback. His eyes narrowed again as he tried to look tough and in charge, but I could tell he'd faltered a little.

"Then they're…"

He trailed off, rubbing his chin. The rest of the company stared at us, confused and impatient to move on.

"The Mainframe is looking for me," I said finally, keenly aware that everyone in the group stood gaping at me. "They must have sent those brutes out to search for me, thinking I might still be in the woods. That's why Terrence had us. His orders from the rebellion were to take me as a negotiation tool to stop the war."

He stared at me hard, trying to figure out if I was lying or not. I stared back, trying not to feel intimidated by the look of steel in his icy eyes.

"She's telling the truth, Eli," said Levi as he scooted through the others towards us. "Capell is a traitor, at least to the true cause. She's trying to take the easy way out of the war."

"Let me get this straight," Eli said, trying to keep calm. "The scientists have been cured and now they're out searching for you on orders from the Mainframe? Forgive me for thinking this is a little hard to believe."

"You need proof?" I said, my temper flaring. "Fine."

I marched over to a small boulder lying on the forest floor and slowly hefted it up. With a grunt, I threw it a good eight or nine feet away. Eli's eyebrows went up in mild surprise.

"That's all great," he replied haughtily, "but how do I know you're not just a weight-lifter?"

"Why would we lie to you?" I exploded, my breath still coming in pants from the exertion. I held up my arms and squeezed the small muscle there. "Do these look like body-builder arms to you? Do you think I've had time to lift weights while on the run from the psychos at the Mainframe?"

"No, but how do I know I'm not being taken in? Maybe you're trying to lead me towards the capitol to turn *me* in."

I hadn't thought of that. Of course the trackers would be wanted by the Mainframe if they were part of the rebellion.

"What about this, then?"

Before anyone could refuse, I grabbed a small pocketknife from Levi's pack and cut the tip of my finger. Everyone started shouting at me, but I simply held my finger up. The blood had already congealed without having had time to dribble down my hand. Eli looked much more startled by this.

"In a matter of hours, not days, it'll heal up. I'm rarely sick, and if I am, I get well quickly. I can run very fast, for long distances. The Mainframe doesn't need me for the cure anymore because a group of rogue scientists managed to get the cure from the others and give it to the Mainframe. Victor Channing wants me for his own revenge, so that he can kill me himself for avoiding his summons and ruining his stupid plans. Does that satisfy your need to know whether or not we're traitors trying to turn you in?"

"Okay, okay," said Eli, holding his hands up in mock surrender. "I believe you. But what do you want me to do about it?"

"For starters, we need to get out of the woods. *Fast*. If Vic's got people cured of akrium injections running around looking for us, it won't take them long. You bought us some time, but those wounds will heal within the day. Vic doesn't know where we got to after we broke my mother out of jail. He probably thinks I stayed in the forest. If they're this far north, they're getting desperate."

Eli looked up and gauged the sun's position. "We'll have to head southwest. The forest stretches south and covers the eastern coast. Quickly."

We turned and followed at a run, no longer able to stay quiet and stealthy. Bushes rustled, twigs cracked as we crashed through the forest in a desperate run. Any walking breaks were limited to five minutes until most of us couldn't take it anymore. Terrence, for one, was practically being dragged, and he didn't have the advantage of using his arms for balance. To my relief, the trees did begin to grow thinner the farther we went. Weak winter sunlight poked through the treetops more frequently as we hurried along. By the time the sun set, we'd reached the outer edges, exhausted and sweat-soaked.

"Break," gasped Eli. We all collapsed onto fallen logs or simply onto the forest floor itself. I gazed beyond the trees at the familiar valley where I'd grown up. I could see the towering buildings of the capitol in the distance. The valley, though urbanized, had its own unique beauty, but not anymore. Now it lay in waste. The ground had been pockmarked and scarred from numerous bombings. Smoke rose from fallen trees and rubble was strewn everywhere. Winter had also taken its toll, robbing the trees of their greenery. The river that ran through the valley churned slowly and coldly, looking gray and dead. The mountains were topped with snow, more gray than white in the dingy smog that hung in the air.

"We'll need to find somewhere to shelter for the night," panted Eli. "We can't be exposed, especially here. The Mainframe has done their best to lay waste to anything aboveground."

"Where are we going to go?" Levi asked, gesturing around at the destruction before us. "Unless we find a cave, which is doubtful, we'll be blown to smithereens if there's a raid tonight."

"I know," Eli grunted. "We have to push on and find somewhere, but we'll have to stay close to the tree-line."

"We have a safe house not far from here," offered one of the other trackers. "But it's closer in to the city."

"That's no good, the city's not safe anymore," Levi replied.

"Well, it may be all we have," said Eli. "We have hideouts all over the forest, but we're on the edge now and can't go back in. I'm not familiar with the valley."

"Besides," said the other tracker, "Nowhere is safe anymore. At least in the city we can duck into someone else's hideout for a while if we can't get to ours."

"Can I point something out?" said Amelia suddenly. We all turned to look at her. "Why would the capitol bomb itself? Their target is the north, remember? So we're probably safer in the city."

"Yes, but you still have rebels trying to assault the city," offered Eli.

"We've seen how weak our resistance is," Amelia countered. "I think the city is our safest bet."

After a while, everyone more or less agreed that we needed to head to the city. I trembled a little at the thought of what Vic would do if he got his hands on me. We had no way to disguise ourselves.

"What if we made for the beach?" I ventured, looking for any option but going directly into the city. "Following the tree line will eventually take us there. It's not so crowded there in the winter and we might be able to find a cove or something to hide in."

Eli deliberated, his pale blue eyes roving across the valley. "I don't know if we'll get as far as the beach, but we can head in a general southwest direction and look for shelter while sticking to the tree line. We can walk, I suppose, since the bounty hunters are hopefully still in the forest."

With that, we ate a quick meal and started off down the edge of the forest, heading south to the sea. A deep uneasiness stirred within me at the thought of being so close to the capitol again, but we had no other choice.

Chapter Fourteen

The terrain grew easier the farther south we headed. Steep, tree-covered hills gradually gave way to gentle grassy slopes. The trees themselves became less thick, more delicate as their bark changed from deep browns and blacks to soft grays and whites.

I felt a slight pang of homesickness all of a sudden. Though I'd grown up in a sooty, dirty city, I'd often looked out beyond the city's borders into the wild around us. A sort of quiet reverence took me every time I'd stared at these trees, longing to live somewhere with clean air and soft, strong dirt beneath my feet instead of concrete. The beach had always been my escape, my refuge in nature. The trees that sloped down towards the ocean had always been part of that longing for and love of all things natural. I'd felt that in the north, but there was something about being home, the place I'd spent most of my life.

"Penny for your thoughts?" asked Levi as he walked beside me.

"Just thinking about home," I replied. "I didn't like the city, but I used to dream about living in these woods, in a little cottage near the beach or something. It feels weird to be here, running for our lives."

He gave me a funny look, making me blush. "I know that sounds cheesy, but I guess it's just ironic," I said. "I always just wanted somewhere peaceful, somewhere away from the chaos of the city, but it doesn't look like I've found so much peace in the forest after all."

"I can relate," he replied, ducking under a low-hanging branch.

"Where did you grow up?"

"Here and there. We moved around a lot. My dad was military."

I felt a bit disappointed, as if he'd cut me short. I'd delved into my past, but he seemed reluctant to bring up his. I thought of Wes again, how I knew so much about him. We'd grown up together, not really hanging in the same crowd or anything, but I knew a lot about him. He knew a lot about me. I wished again that he was here with me. Levi, I realized, was a complete mystery to me.

"Did you like any place in particular?" I ventured.

He paused, looking thoughtful. "I liked this one little town way out in the middle of nowhere. It was real close to the beach, not a lot of people. I used to go snorkeling with my buddies out there. We saw a huge shark one time. It was insane."

His face lit up as he talked. "I had one friend step on some coral and whine like crazy even though he only got a small cut. It didn't even get infected, but you'd have thought he cut his foot wide open."

"I had a friend like that," I replied with a smile, thinking of Cherie and her issues with seeing blood.

"Yeah, he was a pretty good friend." Levi trailed off suddenly, his face drawn.

"You okay?"

He sniffed a little bit. I wondered suddenly if he was crying. "Yeah, fine. He, um, got drafted a couple years later and got killed in combat in the south."

I felt like I'd been knocked out, all the wind pushed out of me.

"I'm…I'm so sorry," I said, feeling like a loser. My heart ached for him as I realized he'd probably seen and been through as much, if not more, than me. I'd been through hell, but at least I'd never lost anyone I knew and cared about.

"It's all right," he replied. "I'm sure he's fine and all, you know, with the big guy upstairs. He was real nice."

A sudden impulse to grab him and kiss him and make all those pains and fears go away seized upon me like a fit of insanity. I shook it off, but thoughts of kissing him continued to haunt me as we trekked farther down the tree line.

The city now loomed before us, stretching out towards the forest like some awful monster claw reaching for a victim. An odd kind of darkness hung about the city, though it obviously hadn't been bombed like the valley farther north.

As I looked out with a feeling of growing apprehension at the city before me, Eli turned back, his face panicked.

"Get into the trees! Hurry!"

With no time to ask what had happened, I followed Levi as he scrambled deeper into the woods.

"Find somewhere to hide!" Eli called in a hushed voice. We ran in crazy zigzags, trying desperately to find a cave, a dugout, anything to hunker down in, but the land had flattened out into one vast tree-filled plain.

"Up in the trees!" Eli hissed desperately, motioning to us as he shinned a tree with inhuman speed.

The trackers were up the trees in no time, but Amelia, Levi and I struggled. I'd climbed trees in a panic before, but it had been a while since I'd done it. The last time had been in a desperate race against the guards at the border gate in the south, but at least I'd known who the enemy was then. As I struggled to grab a branch, a hand grasped mine. I looked up to see Levi. He hauled me onto a thick limb he'd already reached. I looked around and noticed with relief that the others had made it into the trees. Eli held a finger to his lips from two trees away, a signal for absolute silence. He must have sighted some beasts.

The sound of crashing brush came from far away, moving closer all the time. Before long, three men and a woman broke into the clearing below our hiding place.

"It's mine!" screamed one man, vaulting at another running man and tackling him to the ground.

"Get off!" he cried, wriggling like a man possessed to get away from the grip of the other. The man who'd tackled him punched him in the face hard, sending him reeling. The woman came up behind the man and started trying to pry something from his hands. I squinted hard against the sun, but couldn't see what it was they were fighting over.

With a grunt, the man underneath pushed the other man away and scrambled to his feet. The woman grabbed his thick hair before he got far. As the man flew back, a small box soared from his hands, a box of crackers. The woman let go and ran for the box, snatching it up in her claw-like hands. She managed to stuff a fistful into her mouth before the third man snuck up behind her and clubbed her over the head with a rock.

More people rushed into the clearing and began tearing at the others to get to the box of crackers. Women and men alike bit each other, pulled hair, scratched skin and hit with reckless abandon.

I looked at Levi, my mouth agape in horror at the scene before me. His expression mirrored my thoughts, terror and amazement that human beings could act like this.

"Things must be really bad in the city," he whispered. I didn't say anything. I felt glad mom was still safe back up north, but I wondered about Wes's family. They'd still lived there in the city, unless they'd had to flee when he went AWOL. A sick, heavy feeling settled in the pit of my stomach and refused to go away.

Eventually the tide of people moved to a different part of the forest, still fighting like crazed dogs. After a tense hour, Eli finally gave the signal to move out of the trees. My arms and back ached from clinging to the tree.

"We'll have to get to one of the safe houses in the city," he said. "If people are fanning out away from the city, there's probably something major going on in the city to drive them out like that. We might go more unnoticed there than at the beach."

I felt a little stung that my idea was being tossed out, but he had a point. We were much too exposed. I shuddered to think what those people would have done to us if we'd been seen, especially since we had a few rations.

We descended the trees and crept cautiously towards the city limits, keeping a fearful eye out for unfriendly people. All the madness seemed to have moved away, but the forest felt eerily quiet to me, like something wasn't quite right.

"Are you okay?" asked Levi, looking at me with a wary eye. "I mean, going back into the city and all?"

I shrugged. "There's nothing here for me anymore," I replied. "I don't know what it's going to be like, so I can't really say."

His lips pursed. I couldn't tell if he was hurt about my short answer, or just thinking about things. I couldn't think very well since the tightness in my nose had grown. I'd never had a cold that stuck around so long, but now my throat was starting to feel a little raw. I wanted to tell him all this, but couldn't find the energy to explain. Suddenly, more than anything, I just wanted a warm, comfortable bed where I could sleep away all my worries.

Before long, we'd reached the outskirts of the city. We stood up on a high slope looking down at the distant buildings shrouded in early evening fog. If I'd thought the city was bad before, it had now become unrecognizable. Rubble lay strewn across the streets, covered over by shattered glass from broken windows. Smoke rose in hazy rivulets towards the sky, making it hard to breathe. The few people we saw rushed past us, barely noticing us in their haste. Buildings lay in ruin with chunks of drywall or entire walls missing. Doors hung on hinges, trash lined the sidewalks. And above it all, on the massive cliff overlooking the ocean stood the Mainframe building, a dark, cold shadow towering over the ruins that lay all around us. I thought about my old apartment, the Ration Center, school, all the places I used to know, but I knew I didn't want to see them for fear of what I'd find there.

Eli wove his way expertly through the city, ducking into the darkest alleys to avoid contact with the random people remaining in the city. Something terrible had happened here, causing everyone to flee, but I didn't want to think about it.

Within minutes, we'd reached the wealthier district of the city and ducked into a small hardware store. Eli motioned for us to stay back, his ears pricked and alert for any looters. He disappeared down a small staircase under a trapdoor behind the counter, but emerged just minutes later.

"The safe room is still there and stocked," he whispered, though there wasn't another soul on the block. "Hurry."

We followed him down the stairs into a gloomy cellar. When we got to the bottom of the steps, he pulled back a piece of canvas that had been cleverly painted to look exactly like the wall behind it. Until he'd lifted it, I couldn't tell in the dim light that it wasn't part of the wall. We ducked into the door behind it to find a small room furnished with a few cots, boxes, some gallons of water and an oil lamp. I stared at it in wonder, having never seen such a primitive tool.

Eli lit the lantern with some waterproof matches he'd dug up and rummaged in some of the boxes. He found powdered cocoa and some canned beans. A little stove lay hidden in one of the boxes, so we were able to heat the water and the beans. The food tasted good, but made me even wearier than I'd been before.

"Ted and I will take first watch," said Eli. "The rest of you get some sleep. When we've rested, we'll try to figure out our next step."

He didn't have to tell me twice. There weren't enough cots for everyone, but it was immediately decided that Amelia and I would get cots as the only women in the group. A few of the men decided to alternate turns on the remaining cots so everyone could get a comfortable rest.

I lay down on the small cot, relishing the feel of something soft on my back after days of sleeping in the woods. Before my eyes closed, I caught a glimpse of Levi looking at me in the dim lamplight. He looked away shyly when I caught him. I closed my eyes and tried to shut out the feelings of confusion and longing crowding into my brain.

Chapter Fifteen

I woke several hours later, warm and comfortable, not wanting to move. I rolled over onto my stomach and hugged my soft pillow as I stretched my toes and fingers out as far as they would go. My tense muscles slowly uncoiled and relaxed. The only parts of me that didn't feel great at the moment were my nose and throat. An uncomfortable scratchiness at the back of my mouth made it hard to swallow, and my nose had gone from clogged to completely stuffed. I sniffed a few times, trying to clear an airway with not much success. I wondered again why this cold just wouldn't go away. Maybe my body wasn't used to the lower temperatures.

"Hey, sleepyhead," said a voice near my ear. I rolled over again, trying to see the talker through my bleary eyes. Levi gradually came into focus.

"Hey," I replied, my voice still muffled. "What time is it?"

"About eight in the morning. You slept for about twelve hours."

I furrowed my brow, confused. "Have you been on watch this whole time?"

"No. I went to sleep around the same time as you, then I got up for watch two hours ago."

I looked around and noticed, with a sense of self-consciousness, that we were the only ones awake. The others were nestled in thin blankets on the floor or on the other cots, some snoring loudly.

"Any talk about plans?" I asked, trying to shake off my growing awkwardness. I felt acutely aware of my mouth-breathing and weird voice.

"I was asleep for most of anything, but when Eli woke me up, they were talking about possibly doing something to de-stabalize the Invisijets. It's the one thing the south has got over on us. We can't starve them out forever."

"Are you kidding?" I scoffed, instantly forgetting my shyness at the mention of such an absurd idea. "Those things are the pride of Illyria. They'll be under the highest possible surveillance and protection."

"It's just a matter of getting in touch with our buddies in aviation," he

- 77 -

replied. He curled his knees up and leaned his arms on them. "You do know we've got spies all over the country."

I shrugged. "Well, yeah, I figured, but…they wouldn't be in Invisijets. How could they bomb their own comrades?"

"They have to. If they want to be convincing, they have to pretend to be ruthless."

"Ok, if that's the case, then why haven't they done anything by now? They've had all the opportunity in the world. Why pointlessly kill other rebels when they could've destabilized them a long time ago?"

He smirked a little. "You don't know much about this rebellion thing, do you?"

I tried to arrange my face into an indifferent scowl, but the words did hurt a little.

"Hey, I've done more to disrupt the Mainframe that you can imagine," I shot back.

"Oh, I know," he replied, still smiling. "The things I've heard make you sound like some kind of battle-scarred warrior. But I mean you don't know much about being on the inside. You have to play the part convincingly, and only strike when the time is right. The city looks like it's anarchic right now, so maybe it's time to put our plans into action."

"Oh." I had no idea what anarchic meant, so I took the easy way out by not saying anything else. He shifted and stretched his legs as he leaned out against the frame of my cot. The ease with which he teased me, sat close to me and stared at me was starting to unnerve me a little. I couldn't deny that I definitely felt attracted to him, and yet somehow it wasn't the same as Wes. Levi seemed to be getting too comfortable, and not knowing what was happening with Wes and I made it all the more difficult to be around him. If we'd for sure broken up, I might not feel so much guilt and worry, but then again, maybe I'd feel worse.

Shockingly, I realized it had now been almost a month since I'd last seen Wes. I'd lost track of the days in the forest, but it had to be December or close to December by now. The sick feeling of worry crept into my stomach again, and suddenly I missed him terribly. I wanted his reassuring warmth, his strong arms holding me close again. Levi felt like some kind of intruder, a threat to the perfect balance of Wes and I.

Then again, I felt a strange combination of pity and awe when I looked at Levi, this man who'd been through and seen so much. What would draw someone like him to me? He had obviously known and experienced so much more than me. The feeling of confusion overwhelmed me again, making me want to hide in this little bed for the rest of the day.

Eli suddenly appeared, as if from nowhere, and started bustling around making some breakfast. He woke the others, and gradually the room was filled with the buzz of quiet, solemn conversations.

Eli served out small portions of more cocoa and beans. When we'd finished the food, he gave the signal to listen. Everyone stopped talking and turned to him.

"I got in contact with some of our comrades from within the Mainframe Aviation Department. We've got some work to do."

Ever to the point, Eli explained that they needed some kind of distraction to lure the Mainframe officials out of the building in order to give our allies in Aviation time disable the jets. Then they needed time to disappear. The Invisijets were kept very secure in one of the far wings of the Mainframe building. The distraction would have to be something that would draw out those pilots and mechanics not involved in the rebellion, along with other officials in the building.

"It's suicide," said one of the other trackers. Personally, I agreed. There was no way pilots involved in the rebellion would be able to stay in the hangar without raising questions. How would we avoid getting ourselves killed? How on earth would we manage to rescue any rebels within the Mainframe?

"Obviously, the plan is still in the planning stage. We've thought carefully about every possible problem. If any non-rebels remain in the hangars with the jets, they will probably have to be killed or taken prisoner. It's ruthless, but this is war," Eli responded. "Obviously we still have to lay low for a few days until we think of a plan and clear it through our contacts in Aviation. There aren't a lot of us, but they were glad to know we're here. The other rebels have been forced to flee the city in light of the starve-out. The Mainframe has enough supplies to hold out for a few more months, hunkered down the way they are, but they'll slowly start cutting off people lower down the chain. Vic especially will try to keep most of the provisions for himself and his top cronies."

Someone started to ask another question, but was cut off by a low buzzing sound. Eli held up his hand as he picked up a communicator and glanced down at the screen.

"How does he have a communicator?" I asked warily, thinking of Terrence. Terrence sat huddled in a corner, staring venomously at all of us. He made me uneasy. I hoped we'd get rid of him soon.

"Found it in the supplies last night. It's only got untraceable channels on it." Eli spoke in a low voice to whoever was on the other end of the communicator. All of us waited, holding our collective breath. Finally, he clicked off and turned to the rest of us.

"Well, I thought we'd have a little time, but things are worse than we thought," he said grimly. "That was Graham Striker, one of our contacts in the inner circle."

"Inner circle?" said Levi.

"Vic's inner circle," Eli replied.

"We have a contact in his inner circle?" I asked skeptically. "How do we know he's not double crossing us and feeding information directly to Vic?"

"We'd have been dead long ago if that was the case. Graham is a smooth actor, he's worked his way up well for years."

I felt slightly dumb, not knowing that there had been rebels planted in higher government positions in years. Now that I'd heard it, it made complete sense. I'd always wondered why workers in the Mainframe just blindly followed Vic, never questioning the horrible things he did. Most of them were really working for the opposition.

"What did he say?" asked one of the trackers.

"The food situation is getting desperate. Supplies are shorter than previously thought. They're likely to run out in less than a week. We have to pull something off in the next few days in order to get everyone out of there and pull one over on Vic."

"But a move like this could take months to pull off!" Levi interjected. "We can't do a sloppy rush job, we'll all die for sure."

The others nodded and Eli shrugged. "This is our only shot. I've got something in the works, though. And there is some good news."

"Well, that's a relief," said one of the trackers as he rolled his eyes sarcastically.

"We have some other rebels coming up from Epirus. A contingency went down there from up north and managed to convince a whole bunch of Epirians to join us in the fight. They have a bone to pick with Vic anyway, for bombing their capitol and waging war on them."

Levi glanced sideways at me, his face a little red. My heart pounded in my ears and my stomach twisted and churned.

"When will they be here?" I asked quietly.

"Tomorrow morning. They're on the move right now."

Chapter Sixteen

A very strange combination of emotions rushed through my mind all at once; relief to hear that Wes was safe, security knowing that reinforcements were joining us for this insane mission and an overwhelming sense of guilt knowing that Wes and Levi would stand face to face in the same ranks. I looked over at Levi, but he avoided my gaze now, his face turned to the floor, his lips tight.

Eli, not seeming to notice anything, carried on. "We'll need to be abroad in the city tomorrow to meet them at the rendezvous point and take them to our different safe-holds. It's not going to be an easy job, so we'll need everyone's cooperation."

He turned to Terrence. "The prisoner will stay here. He'll have to be guarded. Do I have any volunteers?"

For a moment, I teetered on the idea of volunteering. I didn't particularly want to stay with Terrence, even bound as he was, but the thought of facing Wes made my stomach twist violently.

Before I could make up my mind, however, two of the trackers raised their hands and got the job. Seven of us would be going out to meet the others. It was decided we'd leave before daybreak to avoid drawing too much attention. A large group of wanderers in a deserted city would certainly draw attention if any Mainframe workers were out and about.

The day crawled by slowly in the stuffy store-room. The tightness in my nose and throat had abated somewhat, but still caused discomfort. Why was this cold taking so long to kick? I'd never had anything keep up for so long. I blew my nose into a spare handkerchief in my pocket and leaned back against the wall. I'd just had my third helping of hot cocoa and beans for lunch and it was making weird gurgly noises in my stomach.

"Are you okay?"

Levi came and sat next to me, which surprised me. He'd avoided me for most of the day, and I could guess why.

"All right, I guess," I replied. "I've had a cold coming on for a while, but usually I shake them pretty fast. You know, with my freak powers and all."

His eyes narrowed with worry. "When did you start feeling it?"

"Oh...I guess about the time Terrence showed his true colors. Why?"

He frowned, a look of fear creasing his face. "How long does it take you to get better when you're sick?"

I shrugged. "Usually only a day or two. I've had this for a while now."

His frown grew deeper as he looked down at the floor. "No...he *couldn't* have. Did he? Maybe she did give him some...it wasn't even tested..."

Now I was really starting to panic. Levi seemed to know something I didn't and stared at me like I had cancer. Before I could ask him what he was thinking, he suddenly he got up and marched over to Terrence with long, purposeful strides. In one grasp, he picked him up and hauled him off the floor, holding him nose to nose.

"What did you do to her?" he roared, sending a spray of spit all over Terrence's startled, terrified face.

"What are you talking about, man?"

"I know you did something to her! She's sick!" Levi's face grew so red I could almost feel heat waves coming from him where I sat. The others stared in shocked silence, not even bothering to stop him.

"I didn't-"

"Don't give me that!" he shrieked. "You've been talking to those scientists up at the base, taking things from them, experiments! They were meant for the beasts, and you gave something to her, didn't you? What did Capell make you do?"

Terrence's feet, a few inches off the ground, wind-milled a little. Levi shook him.

"Talk," he commanded through gritted teeth, "or you'll find yourself in a world of pain."

"Allen, come on, step off," said Eli, but even he was silenced by the look Levi gave him.

"I...I was under orders," Terrence stammered, struggling to talk in his awkward position. "It's a form of poison, made from akrium, it makes people sick

- 83 -

from akrium faster, even people who've been cured. One of the scientists, Trent or something, mentioned that one of his guys got away with the cure and leaked it to the Mainframe. He had some kind of beef or somethi-"

"Get to the point," Levi growled.

"Capell told me to give it to Lily if necessary to subdue her so I could bring her in," he gasped as quickly as possible. "I injected her while she slept one night." Levi threw him down in disgust and Terrence hit the floor hard, his head smacking against the wall.

An intense wave of nausea and terror washed over me all at once, making me want to throw up every last baked bean in my stomach. I'd always been strong, healthy and vibrant. Now, suddenly, I felt vulnerable and weak. Had I been permanently damaged?

"What's going to happen to me?" I asked quietly, a tremor shaking my voice.

"Nothing. I'll see to that," said Levi heatedly. "What exactly does this do? How long does she have?"

I looked at Terrence. He rubbed his head where it had hit the wall. "I don't know. They only tested it on one guy. It made him sick, but Capell nabbed some before the trial could be finished. I'm sorry."

He looked at me, his eyes shimmering with tears. He truly looked sorry. For a moment, I felt pity for him, mingled with the horror of knowing just how low Capell had sunk and how many she'd thrown into her little plot. I thought of Wes, sickened to know she'd sent him into combat so he couldn't protest against my being sent out. Mom was already so weak from her ordeal in the Mainframe prison that she couldn't fight to keep me with her. Capell eliminated anyone who would stand in her way. My heart ached for mom. I wished I could communicate telepathically or something with her, to know if she was okay. If Capell had done anything to her....

Tears came spilling down my cheeks though I wished they wouldn't. Everyone stared shamelessly, making me even more upset. I wanted to hide or run away or something, anything to get away from all the staring eyes.

"Well....ah...um..." stuttered Eli. "This, um, changes our plans a little."

"What do you mean?" Levi said flatly.

"Hey, easy," Eli replied, putting his hands up defensively. "I just mean that we need to look out for her, that's all. Maybe it was a bad idea to bring her down here."

"Well, we don't exactly have the provisions to send her back up north to see if they can reverse what he did to her," said Ted, Eli's right-hand man. "Besides, maybe she'll be of help to us."

"You better not be insinuating that we use her as bait, like this trash tried to do," Levi growled, rounding on Ted and using his hand to point to Terrence.

"I'm not. Get a grip. I'm just saying she's been in the Mainframe before. She knows the layout. At the very least, she grew up here. She could act as guide."

Seriously, did everyone know about my past? Was nothing sacred anymore?

"I'm kind of standing right here, while you're talking about me," I pointed out, my voice still muffled and sniffly from crying.

Eli stood thoughtfully for a moment, his chin resting on his hand, deep in thought. "How do *you* feel about all this, Lily? Would you be strong enough to still help?"

"I…yeah, I guess," I replied, feeling a little unsure, especially since everyone was still staring at me.

"You don't have to do anything, Lily. You can even stay here and rest if you want," Levi said, his voice softening a little. Eli looked a little annoyed to have someone else playing at being the leader, even if it was only on my behalf.

"I don't really know what to do," I said honestly. All I really wanted was to crawl into a hole and die at this point.

"Well, if you feel well enough, Lily, we could really use your help. You're definitely capable, and your knowledge of the Mainframe building would be invaluable," Eli said. "But I don't want you to do anything you feel uncomfortable with, especially after such upsetting news."

I paused, scrambling for an answer I didn't have. I just wanted to lie down, especially now that a searing pain had started shooting through my head. I could sit here all day with the two guards and Terrence, but the idea repulsed me. This stuffy room was too much.

"I can help, but…I'd like to be paired with Levi, if that's okay," I asked, surprising myself. Levi's face lit up with pleased surprise before he arranged it carefully back into his neutral grimace.

"No problem. That helps us tremendously, thank you," said Eli formally, as if he were talking to his boss. "We'll be all in a group tomorrow when we meet the allies from the south, of course, but we'll put you two on a team to lead some of the others to our safe points to await further orders."

Thankfully, everyone seemed to go back to their own business after that. I dried my face as Levi sat next to me.

"Partner, eh?" he said, unable to keep a grin off his face.

"Well…you're the only one I really know. Or trust. Well, I trust Amelia too, but I don't know her as well as I know you."

Shut up, stop rambling, I told myself, suddenly feeling a bit self-conscious.

He struggled again to not look too pleased. "I won't let anything happen to you, I promise. We'll figure this out somehow. I'm not sure what that idiot injected you with, but hopefully it was still a trial experiment that won't do much."

I nodded, still feeling a little too overwhelmed to talk. I felt better knowing Levi would stay with me, but I also couldn't shake the growing feeling of guilt and doubt growing in my mind.

Chapter Seventeen

By the next morning, I knew the chemical in my body was starting to take more of an effect. A strange tightness hung heavy in my lungs, making it laborious to breathe. I kept quiet, not wanting to alarm Levi and the others. I'd had the poison in me this long with little effect, so what was a few more days?

I gathered my things up quietly while Levi instructed the guards on what to do with Terrence. It was too risky to move him so he'd be jailed and guarded in the little room. I felt another surge of pity towards him. He had looked truly sorry when he admitted what he'd done, yet the horror of it was too fresh. I still couldn't bear the fact that he'd been so kind to me in the beginning, then purposely shot me with something to make me weak. It made the betrayal all the worse.

"Ready to go?" asked Levi as he sidled up next to me.

"Think so," I replied shortly. My moods seemed to go up and down with him. One minute, I really thought about leaving Wes and my feelings for him behind and giving myself over to Levi, and the next I wanted nothing to do with him. The emotions churned in my mind over and over again, making me feel sick. I knew I loved Wes. And realizing the true reason why he'd been sent away took the edge off of our last moments together. Though he'd been duped by that rat in heels, he had gone south for a noble cause.

Levi took the hint and let me simmer. After everyone had gathered their gear, Eli gathered us round for one last instruction.

"We've got to get to the rendezvous point as quickly as possible. Since Lily knows the city best," he said, pausing to look at me, "she will act as guide. I know the tracker's hideouts, but I don't know my way around the city very well."

"Whoa, hang on, I don't even know where we're going yet," I interjected.

"I was just getting to that," he said, giving a wink. "Do you know where Lander's Beach is?"

I gasped involuntarily. Wes. Wes had given the rendezvous location. Somehow I just knew it. I felt immediately like I'd been punched in the stomach. Lander's Beach was *our* beach, the place we'd formally met, the place we'd first kissed...

"Lily," said Eli, looking at me like I'd been shouting gibberish. "You with us?"

"Yeah, sorry," I replied. "I do. I can get us there."

"Good. Let's get moving."

Someone found some dried fruit and nuts in a box, so we ate that for breakfast. It was certainly a nice break from the beans. I wanted desperately to ask if Wes had been the one to communicate with Eli, but felt too weird about it. I kept my mouth shut, trying to stomach my food without throwing it back up with my nerves. The pressure on my chest definitely didn't help.

We snuck slowly from the hidden room, closing the door and hanging the painted canvas carefully back in place. Levi took my hand, but I shook him away. I knew I was being rude, but my nerves couldn't handle it.

"Here," said Eli, turning and facing us with a lump of coal in hand. He began smudging it all over our faces and hands. When he was done, he took a pair of scissors to strategic places on our clothing, fraying the cut edges to make them look worn and old. He didn't really have to do much work on Levi, Amelia and I, though. Our clothes looked disgusting since we'd been wearing them since the beginning of our mission.

"What are you doing, man?" asked one of the trackers. Eli rolled his eyes.

"You should know. We can't travel in a pack like this without attracting attention. If anyone spots us, hopefully they'll think we're a random group of refugees."

Eli led us quickly to the front door of the shop and motioned for us to wait.

"How are you feeling?" Levi whispered.

"I'm fine."

"Lily..."

"Look, I'm fine, really," I said, looking him in the face for the first time that morning. I immediately wished I hadn't. He had a look of sadness in his eyes, a look that plainly said he felt his time was running short. Wes was coming. We both knew it, and we both knew I belonged with him.

- 88 -

"Thanks," I whispered, giving his hand a quick squeeze. I dropped it as quickly as I had grabbed it and followed Eli as he motioned us out the door.

"Keep your weapons stowed," Eli cautioned. He had wrapped his bow in some small, spare blankets from the hidden room. It looked like a ragged bundle on his back. "Act like you're fleeing. Lily, I need you up here to guide."

I moved up next to Eli with Levi right behind me. I directed him quietly down side streets and alleyways, making our way west towards the coast. My breathing turned from small pants to ragged gasps as we wound through the complicated city maze. My lungs felt about to explode, but I kept quiet. Luck was with us, as we only ran into the occasional hungry straggler lying on the sidewalk, too weak from hunger to move. Eli brushed past them impatiently, trying to look like he was in a hurry.

"Can't we at least give them some of our provisions?" I hissed. "They're starving to death!"

"We can't draw attention," he whispered back. "We help one, and they'll all swarm us." He looked down at me, an expression of sadness on his face. I couldn't deny that he was right. "Look, I don't like it either, but we have to keep moving. We can't do anything that a refugee wouldn't do. They would hoard whatever supplies they had and keep moving."

Everything made sense, but it still bothered me. A few streets further, I halted and realized I'd unconsciously led the group to Cherry Lane, where my old apartment complex stood. For a moment, I stopped and looked up at our old balcony, or what was left of it. The front half of the building had been completely torn away by who knew what.

"What's the matter?" asked Eli briskly. I could tell he was annoyed by the delay, but I couldn't move. Someone was up there, I noticed, sitting on the neighboring balcony. I took a few steps closer, then stopped, feeling an odd sort of ringing in my ears. Thelma, our old neighbor, sat propped against the wall like some kind of odd rag doll, her eyes dull and lifeless. She clutched a watering can in her hand. I remembered saying hi to her occasionally. I didn't really know her. All I knew was that she loved flowers, and kept some in pots on her balcony.

"Go on to the rendezvous," I said, still transfixed and horrified.

"We need you to guide us," Eli replied, looking around nervously. "We don't know where to go."

I pointed. "Cherry runs west until it hits the frontage road. Take the frontage road to the south to the beach. Lander's Beach is at the end. You can't miss it."

"We shouldn't split up," Levi insisted.

"We'll catch up," I argued, starting to get annoyed myself. "Levi will stay with me."

Levi got that semi-triumphant look on his face again, irritating me. Didn't he realize the shock and pain I felt, seeing Thelma like that?

I shrugged off my aggravation and turned to Eli. "You'll find a signpost at the beach," I offered. "The pier is a short distance away. They'll probably be there."

"What is the big deal, anyway? What are you doing?"

I shut my eyes tight and opened them again, trying to hide my tears. "Just go! We'll meet you, okay?"

"Fine," he shot back, turning on his heel and motioning for the others. They marched down according to my directions. I watched them for a while, indifferent, unfeeling. I couldn't figure out my mood. I'd been neighbors for years with Thelma, but never really thought too much about her. Now…now I wished I had.

I crept up the damaged staircase towards my old apartment on the top floor. Levi followed dutifully, though I could tell he was confused. Thankfully, he knew better than to ask questions right now.

I glanced at my apartment when we reached the top of the stairs, grieved by what I saw. The walls had been blown apart. Our scant furniture lay tumbled around the room, as if torn apart by a tornado. The tile we'd scraped and saved for and laid so carefully in the kitchen had been ripped up and scattered through the rooms. The carpet lay stained with things fallen from the cupboards. The cupboards themselves looked as if someone had tried to rip them from the walls. Mom's old recliner lay tipped on its side, the stuffing falling out of a huge tear.

"This is where I grew up," I said simply, tears falling gently onto my dirty, rumpled shirt. Thelma's apartment didn't look much better than mine and mom's. I knelt gently next to her and eased her body to the ground. I closed her eyes and arranged her hands over her chest. Next to her were a few of her flower pots, one of the plants miraculously surviving the raid or whatever had happened here. A lone flower, wilted in the winter wind, sat on one of the leaves. I lightly plucked it off and arranged it beneath her hand.

"Was she…was she someone you knew?" Levi asked quietly.

"She was my neighbor," I replied, surprised by how robotic and numb I sounded. "I didn't know her very well, but I...I couldn't leave her like that."

Levi rested his hand gently on my shoulder. I let it be. The warmth felt good to my cold body. I knew I was missing Wes, but somehow seeing him just didn't matter anymore. Nothing mattered anymore. Thelma was dead because of me. This defenseless old woman died just because she was neighbors with a freak.

"We need to get going," I said, my voice still robotic. I stood up and made my way down the rickety staircase, not caring if I fell.

"Lily..."

I turned on my heel and stopped. "Don't. Just save it. This is all my fault. Thousands are dead because of me."

"That's not true," Levi offered. "You know it's not."

"I don't know what's true anymore." My lips trembled. "If I'd just given myself up and gone to Vic in the first place, none of this would have happened."

"Don't say that!" Levi took my hands in his. "This war was always meant to happen. You just happened to be a piece in Vic's game."

I knew what he was trying to say, but I didn't want to face it and work through it just yet. I turned and headed down the street, trying to forget the awful pressure in my chest.

"Lily!" shouted Levi.

"Just don't..."

"Get down!" he hissed, grabbing me by the waist and pulling me into a shadowy alley.

"What're you-"

He gently pressed his hand to my mouth and pointed with the other. I followed his gesture and gasped. Two Mainframe soldiers rushed down the street, looking in and around my old apartment complex.

Chapter Eighteen

Levi slowly lowered his hand from my mouth and put a finger to his lips. He didn't have to tell me twice. Sheer terror kept my mouth shut.

The soldiers rummaged around on the balcony, casually moving Thelma like she was a sack of potatoes. I bit my tongue to keep myself from screaming at them, telling them to leave her alone. My fists clenched angrily at my sides, and the now-familiar tide of anger rose within me. Levi glanced back at me and gave a little start. He'd probably noticed my eyes.

"Are you sure you saw someone here, Davis?" asked one of the guards in a bored voice.

"Two people, actually," another voice grunted. "A girl and a guy."

"The city is emptying out anyway, why does it matter?"

"One of them could be her."

"I seriously doubt that. If she knows what's good for her, she'll steer clear. Vic'll have her head on a silver platter."

"She's not the smartest person from what I've heard. She may come back here with the rebellion."

I ground my teeth furiously and breathed through my nose, willing myself to calm down. They were obviously talking about me, and I knew they didn't know anything about what had really happened the past few months, but it made me mad all the same.

"We should check this apartment, but this old broad's in the way."

"Chuck her over the side then," said one, waving his hand carelessly.

That did it. Before I could think twice, before I could resist my irrational urge, I rushed out from the alley and headed towards the soldiers, ready to rip into them. I felt Levi grabbing for me, but I brushed him off. I'd had enough. If they could act that callous about someone's death, someone who'd always been good and kind, then they deserved to die.

"Lily!" Levi hissed. "No!"

I kept running.

"Hey…" started one of the guards, then stopped midsentence. I didn't bother to look at the shock on his face. In one swift movement, I was up the stairs, my lungs burning in protest. The guard trying to move Thelma found my fist buried into his nose. With a high-pitched yelp of pain, he crumpled to the ground on the balcony. I kicked him in the ribs for good measure, then turned on the other guard. He leveled a gun at my head. That stopped me for a minute. I took a few deep breaths.

"Go on, then," I hissed. "I'm sure Vic will be so happy that you killed his number one target. I'm sure he wants that pleasure for himself, but you go on…"

For a moment, fear flickered in his eyes. It had been a well-known fact that Vic would kill anyone who messed with his plans.

"You're coming with me," the guard growled.

I looked around desperately, starting to feel panic for the first time. I noticed the stairs going down the opposite side had been damaged somehow. A few of the stairs were cracked through the middle. If I played my cards right, I could get the guard to step on a bad stair and fall.

"Fine," I replied evenly. I walked towards the opposite stair.

"Davis," the guard barked. "Get up."

With a groan, the other guard staggered to his feet and leaned heavily on the railing as we made our way to the staircase. I moved carefully on the first step and it held. The next one was cracked, but if the guard saw me skip it, he'd know it was bad. Gingerly, I stepped to the far right of the step and held my breath. It didn't give way. I stepped onto the next step, more confident and waiting for the guard to tumble. Out of the corner of my eye, to my dismay, he'd noticed my action and mimicked it. I continued down the stairs, sagging under the weight of finally being defeated.

"Uuuuugggooooaaaaaahhh!"

A loud crash sounded behind me. I stopped and turned, unable to help myself, and saw to my delight and horror that Davis, the guard I'd injured, had toppled on the bad step. In a split second, he bashed into the other guard and the gun went flying onto the pavement at the bottom of the staircase. I slipped to the far left of the step and gripped the rail as the two tumbled past. As soon as they hit the pavement, I jumped the last four or so steps and started to run.

"Don't let her get away!" shouted the guard who'd held the gun.

"You get her!" shouted the other, the one I'd injured. "My arm is broken!"

I ran for all I was worth, feeling the adrenaline of escape once again. Then, without warning, I tripped on loose rubble and fell forward onto the pavement. I heard an odd tap near my nose as it bonked the concrete. Stars popped before my eyes and it took an unusually long time to draw breath again. Pain rocketed from my shoulder throughout my body, and something warm and wet seeped down my back, soaking my shirt.

Blood, I realized with a shock. *My blood.*

From nowhere, Levi appeared and scooped me up. He kept on running in one fluid motion, as if I were a five pound sack of flour and not a full-grown woman. Blood seeped steadily from my arm, making my head pound.

"Levi..." I whispered, trying to nestle myself closer to him. "I..."

"Don't talk," he replied. "Save your strength until we find a safe place."

I gave up, too tired and pained to argue back. I leaned my head against his chest and let the blackness take me.

I woke after what felt like hours, feeling a stiff kind of pain in my arm. I looked down to see a rough bandage of sheets bound securely around the wound on my shoulder. Levi sat near my head, propped against a concrete wall, one of four, his face turned down, shoulders slumped. He was asleep.

I sat up slowly and looked around. We were in some kind of metal shed. Behind me to the right was some kind of metal roller door. A storage locker. A small flashlight sat in one corner, giving the room a little light, and the roll top door had been lifted a crack to let in some fresh air. I was lying on some kind of sheet on the hard concrete floor.

"You're awake."

I turned to see Levi, his smile wide with relief.

"Where are we?"

"Some storage lockers," he replied. "I didn't have anywhere else to go on short notice, but luckily the one guard broke an arm or something in the fall. He couldn't run very fast after me. They won't find us any time soon."

"Are we still in the city?"

"The outskirts." He fell silent for a moment. "What on earth were you thinking?"

I shrugged, sending a burst of pain through my arm and forcing me to lay back. Levi frowned and ran a hand softly over the bandage.

"I'm sorry," I replied through gritted teeth. "I don't always think before I act."

"I noticed," he replied with a smirk. I rolled my eyes and tried to keep the pain off my mind. Tears tried to creep from my eyes, but I forced them away.

"It's ok," he laughed. "We're safe now. I've decided I kind of like your rash impulsiveness."

I felt myself blush like a silly school girl, but at least the tears went away. I didn't want to cry in front of him. I noticed that he reddened a little too.

"What happened?" I asked, trying to change the subject.

"The guy who didn't get hurt shot at you," he replied, looking away. "I knocked him out. He only grazed your shoulder, so the bullet didn't go in."

I stared down dazedly at my shoulder. I'd never been shot before, and it scared me more than I wanted to admit.

"Um…do you want something to eat?" Levi asked. He must have noticed that I was freaking out a little. I agreed a little too eagerly, thinking the same thing. I didn't want to think about the fact that I'd actually been shot.

I took some jerky, though it tasted leathery and dull in my mouth. I put it down after chewing for a bit, too flustered to really eat it.

"Do you want some water?" he asked, holding out a small, plastic bottle. I reached for it and brushed his fingers accidentally with mine. He dropped the bottle, but I barely noticed. Before I could quite register what happened, he had reached out and gently caressed my cheek. I leaned into the touch and closed my eyes, elated and terrified all at once. He leaned in and kissed me softly, questioningly, as his hand moved gently down my arm. I ran my fingers through the thick hair on the back of his neck, pulling him closer.

And then, like some weird daydream, Wes's face flashed across my mind. I remembered all too clearly his laugh, his touch, his *kiss*. Everything about him. And suddenly, I knew I couldn't be with Levi. I could be happy, very happy with him, but I needed Wes the way I needed air. I pushed Levi away, shame burning in my stomach like hot tar. I couldn't quite look at him, but I knew he looked as confused as I felt.

"I…I can't, we can't," I whispered, the words tumbling awkwardly from my dry tongue. "I'm…I have someone. I'm sorry, I don't know what happened, but I can't…we can't…"

I knew I was babbling like an idiot while Levi just stared at me, obviously hurt.

"Who, Wes? The guy who deserted you? You really think you're his priority, Lily?"

I bit my lip, angry and sad at the same time. It was the question I'd always asked myself. I didn't like the way Levi spat his name, and yet he did have a point. Wes opted for the mission instead of being with me. Then again, could I really blame him? He probably thought that if the war was over, we could finally stay together in peace and actually date instead of hiding and running all the time.

"I know it seems like I'm crazy for still wanting to be with him," I started slowly, "but he's been there for me in the past. I think he took the mission to help me. It's…hard to explain."

I looked up at him, afraid of what I'd see, but Levi stared at the ground. He shook his head in disgust as he slunk away from me. He picked up the water bottle and put it down roughly on the floor next to me.

"In case you get thirsty," he muttered. I lay back on the sheet, miserable, confused, angry. He'd just saved my life, and I'd just ripped out his heart. A large part of me felt pain of the worst kind, knowing Levi longed for me the way part of me longed for him.

Levi picked up a communicator, clearing his throat loudly. "We need medical assistance. Lily's been hurt, but she's able to move now."

"Where are you?" came a voice on the other end, a voice I recognized as Eli's.

"Some storage locker. I don't know what it's called, but it's got a pelican on the sign. Outskirts of the city, west side, near the beach. Number fifteen."

My heart hammered as he talked. That meant we weren't far from the rendezvous point. Wes was probably within a couple miles of me.

"We're on it. One of my medics will be there shortly."

"Good. Be on the lookout for enemy soldiers. We ran into a few on the way here."

Chapter Nineteen

Pain like I'd never felt before tore through my body, making me shivery and weak. Tears flowed freely from my eyes as I bit down on the sleeve of my shirt to keep from crying out.

"Almost there, hold on, Lily."

The voice came as if from far away. My strangled sobs burned my throat. I desperately wanted the water bottle next to me, but I couldn't lift my arm to grip it.

"Okay, you're all patched," came the voice of the medic. He'd met us in the little storage locker with his bag of gear. His quick hands cut the end of the stitches he'd neatly sewn, sending another wave of pain and nausea coursing through me.

At last I was able to rest, the wound cleaned and bound with a bandage. I felt a strange sort of ache as I watched the medic dispose of Levi's homemade sheet bandage.

The medic prepped a syringe and stuck it into my arm, making me gasp. "This is for the pain," he said kindly. "It'll help you sleep."

I was out before he'd finished his sentence. The blackness welcomed me like a warm blanket. I sank happily into oblivion, glad to leave my worries behind.

I woke again later to find myself on a small cot in the corner of a large room covered with broken shelves and littered with all sorts of strange items; postcards, trinkets, purses, knick-knacks. An oil lamp burned in one corner, giving off a faint glow. I sat up and saw the faint glow of light through a window, but it had been covered with some kind of black cloth.

"She's awake."

I looked around and noticed the people around me for the first time. They sat in the midst of the mess in a huddle. I recognized Eli and his group of trackers, a small group of men I didn't know, and Levi. He sat hunched in a corner, staring at the floor, his lips tight.

"Lily," said a soft voice. I caught my breath. There he was, breaking free of the huddle and rushing towards me.

"Wes," I whispered. He kissed me, and I wanted to enjoy it, but I couldn't shake the feeling of my betrayal. He wouldn't kiss me so eagerly if he knew.

"I'm sorry," he said, scooting back a little. "I know you're not feeling good. I just…I'm glad to see you."

"I'm glad to see you too," I replied hollowly. "But…can we talk somewhere else? A little more private?"

I knew if I didn't tell him now, I never would and the guilt would haunt me forever. He nodded and hurried over to the group in the middle of the room. Eli and the others nodded and waved him away. They'd probably already talked about what would happen when I woke up.

"Do you feel like walking?" Wes asked when he came back.

"Yeah, I'll be okay," I replied, knowing he probably wouldn't want to even touch me when he found out what happened. Levi's lips pulled even tighter as he watched us walk away.

We left the building, Wes looking both ways before we crept out of the door. I recognized the place instantly. We'd come to the old abandoned pier on Lander's Beach. They'd made a makeshift headquarters out of what used to be the gift shop at the end of the long walkway. I gazed down towards the ocean, remembering with pain our first kiss here.

We walked down the boardwalk and onto the sand. Wes led me to a sandy area next to the pilings of the pier. We sat down far enough from the water that the tide wouldn't wet our feet. Ordinarily, I'd just go ahead and poke my feet in the water, but it had to be December now and the water would be freezing.

"I'm so glad you're okay," Wes burst out, as if he'd been wanting to talk for a long time, but held back for my sake. The realization made me feel sick to my stomach. He'd never once stopped caring about me. He'd never thought we'd broken up. And we never had. How was I stupid enough not to see that? We'd had one ridiculous argument, that was all. I dug my knuckles into my forehead, trying to knead away the ache.

"I've thought about you non-stop since we left. I got in contact with some of the people I met in Epirus and they were a little skeptical at first, but they said they'd help. They really think the tide has turned and that we have a chance…"

I let his words wash over me like the water over the sand, picking up on some things but mostly concentrating on the terrible news I had to give. Would he be able to overlook it? Would he forgive me? If the situation were reversed, I didn't know whether I could forgive and forget so easily. But I couldn't keep it a secret forever. I couldn't keep it a secret at all, not from him.

"Wes," I interrupted, looking him full in the face for the first time. His enthusiasm faded in the wake of my seriousness.

"Hey, sorry Lily, I got a bit carried away," he laughed nervously. "Are you okay? What's been going on up here?"

I took a deep breath and let it out slowly. "I um…well…"

I swallowed hard, grasping for the right words. Wes laced his fingers into mine, gazing at me with a concern so deep I literally felt my heart break.

"Well…I, um…I've just been pretty much the worst girlfriend ever," I replied, a sob ripping from my throat as I said it. Wes's face went from a little tired to downright pale.

"What happened?" he asked slowly.

"Capell asked me to go on a supply run with Levi and a couple of the others and…one of the guys betrayed us, was going to turn me in instead, and…well, long story short, Levi and I kind of ended up on our own."

I stopped and swallowed again, wishing I had a cold drink of water to clear my aching throat and head.

"Oh." Wes let go of my hand. "Well. That explains a lot."

"It just happened once…he kissed me, I mean. I'm…I'm so sorry, Wes."

He looked at me, his face calm. "Did you kiss him back?"

"Um…I…"

He got up and brushed the sand from his pants. "It's okay, you don't need to tell me. You've said enough."

"Wes," I said, struggling to my feet, "I…I did, I'm sorry, but then I thought of you and I knew I couldn't be with him that way. I love you, Wes. More than anything."

He kept walking. Tears streamed more thickly down my face, strangling my voice as I stumbled to keep up with him.

"Please believe me!" I choked out.

He turned to face me and I noticed with a shock that tears ran down his face too. I'd never seen him cry before.

"I loved you too, Lily."

Loved?!?

He turned on his heel and walked swiftly back to the pier, not looking back. I crumpled onto the sand, feeling overcome with shame and anger at myself. My throat burned, making me feel raw all over. I lay back on the chilly sand, not caring that rain had begun to fall and soaked me slowly to the bone.

Somehow I fell asleep. I woke sometime later to see that it had come to the blackest part of the night. I looked around, disheveled and disoriented. I slowly rubbed away the sand that coated my face and the cracks in my ears while I'd slept. As I sat up, cold and sore, I thought again of Wes. I glanced at the gift shop on the pier. The windows were dark, but I couldn't see anything through the blackout curtains.

I looked out at the black, churning water and had a strange, sudden desire to walk out and let the waves wash over me. I wanted to sink to the depths of the sea and never show my wretched face again. For all I knew, both Levi and Wes might have decided I wasn't worth it and convinced the company to move into the city for the final assault, leaving me behind.

I took a step towards the water. Wes would never forgive me. The damage had been done. Levi hated me too, for choosing him. I'd caused this entire war. Everything was all my fault.

I took another step. I thought of mom. What would she do without me? Who would take care of her? I faltered on the next step. I'd worked so hard to keep mom alive. She'd done the same for me, keeping my strength hidden, shuffling us around, knowing I'd be a target. She'd lost her husband, my father. She'd worked herself into sickness trying to support us both.

I paused, tears running down my face once more. I couldn't do something so cowardly, not when mom needed me. Somehow, someday, I'd push through this. The war could still end. We could still win. Wes would phase gradually out of my life, become a distant memory. Maybe I'd even meet someone else. Maybe I'd take mom and we'd go far away from this place, into the north where we'd never have to face pain or heartache again.

A sudden wave of dizziness overtook me, making me sway on my feet. My knees hit the wet sand, making a strange sucking noise. A frigid wave of water overtook me, swirling around my waist, making me gasp. I fell onto my side and rolled onto my back, the stars in the sky swimming in and out of my vision. Water washed around my head, making me sick when it sloshed into my mouth.

And then, I was lifted, yanked from the wet, sucking sand and lifted away. Someone held me close and felt my forehead.

"She's burning up. Get the medic!" called a panicked voice.

The voice sounded so familiar, but the water in my ears clogged and muted every noise around me. As my vision blackened around the edges, I looked up and caught a glimpse of his face in the starlight.

Wes.

Chapter Twenty

A slow, steady rhythm shook me from my deep sleep. I sat up groggily and looked around. Windows, a blur of grayish-green, fluorescent lights, hard, uncomfortable plastic beneath me. A train.

"You okay?"

I turned around to the sound of his familiar, steady voice and felt my heart rise in relief. Wes sat opposite me, an unreadable look on his face. I stretched my legs and touched my feet to the floor. I'd been put up in a makeshift bed of train seats. The arm rests had been lifted so I could lie somewhat comfortably.

"I guess so," I murmured, but even as I said it I knew something was terribly wrong. My stomach lurched as the train jolted suddenly on its tracks. My head spun. The pain of…whenever I'd last been conscious came shooting down my back. A violent cough ripped from my lungs, making my entire body shudder. Wes sat up, alert and (dare I hope) concerned.

"What time is it?" I asked, trying to be casual and play off the pain I felt.

Wes consulted his watch. "Two in the afternoon."

My eyes widened in surprise. "How long have I been out?"

A strained, sort of grunting laugh escaped him. "A *long* time. The medic kept you under his care and stabilized your fever for a few hours, but it wasn't enough. We knew we'd have to get you back to Trent. It took about three hours to get our car across barricades to the city train station. They got us on the train around ten a.m. Took some maneuvering considering the trains have been a sore point in this whole conflict. In the end we had to use some hefty negotiation with the capitol guards. They didn't put up much of a fight when they saw our heat."

He nudged a handgun next to his leg and smirked. "You were out for all of that. And I'm wiped out, so now that you're up, I might catch a few." He sounded different, but I couldn't pin down what it was. He didn't smile, but he didn't seem as furious as he'd been at the beach.

I leaned back against the seat, covered in sweat. My whole body felt on fire, but it felt so good to be in a warm train car, sitting with Wes, who somehow tolerated my presence. Then again, maybe he'd hit his head and forgotten all the misery I'd put him through. Or maybe he was in denial.

"Didn't they have guns too?" The question kind of popped out of me, even though I'd intended to keep quiet. He opened his eyes and shrugged.

"Nope. All arms have gone to protect the Mainframe. The tide has officially turned."

I sat up straight. "You're kidding!"

"Nope," he repeated. "All the people closest to Vic are hunkered down. Eli's working on a plan with the Epirus contingency as we speak. The people inside the Invisijet unit at the Mainframe disabled the jets and got out with only a few casualties. Things are finally going our way."

"What is the contingency going to do?"

"Well, phase one of the new plan is up to us," he replied. "Our job is to get back to rebel headquarters and dismantle Capell's hierarchy and get you better. Step two is to get the sickness formula that you were injected with, put it into tranquilizer form so we can shoot the rebel scientists who've been cured and slow them down. Step three is to deliver them to our agents stationed around the Mainframe. It's being guarded by those scientist brutes, so once we take them down, we have easy access, especially if Trent can make something a little more fast-acting. Then our path to Vic is clear."

I pulled my knees up to my chest. "Sounds risky."

"It is. But that's why they sent us. We have the best shot at getting rid of Capell, especially you."

He looked away suddenly, his face tired and wan. I couldn't figure out if he was angry to have to travel with me, or if he just didn't care anymore, or if he was somewhere in between.

"Wes...are you, um...well..."

He leaned forward. "Am I still mad at you?"

I looked down at my toes and nodded, then looked back up as he let out a slow breath. His expression pained me, so I could only imagine what was going through his mind just then. I'd basically put him on the spot and asked if he still loved me, which, I realized, was what I really wanted to know. I felt suddenly naked, as if I'd laid out everything about myself for his approval. I glanced down at my feet again, uncomfortable, my cheeks burning, wishing I hadn't seen what I'd seen or said what I'd said.

"I…was hurt. Very hurt. And surprised. I didn't think anything like that would ever happen to us."

I bit my lip, forcing back my tears. I didn't want to cry. I couldn't cry. Not now. I needed a clear head, or as clear as it could get with how sick I felt.

"But…" he continued, "I sat and thought about it while the others made plans and I realized you must have felt pretty abandoned at that point. I know I rushed off on this mission, but I needed to straighten some things out with a good friend there, one who probably thought I'd turned traitor on him."

That was new. A flash of anger burst within me.

"Why didn't you just tell me that in the first place then?" I asked, trying to keep anger from my voice.

He rubbed the back of his neck with his hand. "I…I don't know, Lil. It was just something I felt I needed to do. I felt bad for kind of just leaving him there when he'd trusted me and helped me stay out of prison. Some really terrible things happened when I was in Epirus, and I wanted to explain to him why I took off."

I sat back, my hackles down again. He had always gotten kind of a haunted look when I'd asked him about Epirus. Shame mixed with understanding as I realized once again that he'd never truly forgotten me or tried to hurt me.

"Besides," he continued, "I really thought that an alliance would help turn the tide. And it did. Since I'd been down there, along with a couple other guys who escaped after the war, we were the best shot for that kind of mission."

I nodded, impressed by the fact that he could calm down and reason so quickly. If he'd cheated on me, I'd probably either punch the hussy he'd kissed, or do something desperate and crazy in a fit of depression. My love for him suddenly grew immensely, making my heart ache. How would he ever love me again if he felt he couldn't trust me?

"I know," I replied slowly. "Mom told me that too. I guess I just lost it or something. I didn't know after the last time we talked if we were broken up or if you still cared about me or…"

I trailed off, feeling like scum again. How could I have ever questioned him? Wes had always been loyal to me, even in school. We'd never talked that much growing up, but he'd always been polite and kind. He'd always treated me like a person, not the weird girl whose mom was dying. And somehow, finally, we'd come together. We were always meant to be together. Why had I lost sight of that?

I looked into his face and was startled to see an earnest sort of heartache there as he stared at me.

"I will always care about you, Lily. Even if our relationship does end. Someone whose been through what you've been through deserves that much."

I began to sob, no longer caring about holding it in. He was so good, so pure, I knew that I didn't deserve him. A poisonous rage welled up within me, hatred of myself and what I'd done. I nodded mutely, trying to choke back my emotion.

"I love you, Wes," I said, my voice coming out small and squeaky. "I'm so sorry."

I lay down and curled up into a little ball, covering myself tightly with the small blanket he'd given me even though my body felt like an inferno. Too ashamed to talk anymore, I wrapped my arms around myself and chanced a glance at Wes. He stared at the ceiling, blinking rapidly. I closed my eyes. Even the sight of him made me feel horrible. After a while, I heard him shifting around and figured he had lain down to try to get some sleep. The train ride to the north was a long one, passing through several cities. The train stopped in each one, even though no one rode the train much anymore in open warfare. We had the whole car to ourselves.

I wondered vaguely if I'd ever be able to sleep again with all the guilt and pain raging through me, but somehow I fell into a fitful doze full of awful nightmares.

We both woke around the same time a few hours later. The reinforcements down south had managed to pilfer some emergency food to send us with. We ate a quiet meal of crackers and other non-perishables. He drank a swig of water from a small bottle and offered it to me. I took it gratefully, the water putting out some of the fire that raged within me.

As day faded into night, the train began to slow, then screeched to a halt in a small town that I recognized as the rendezvous point of my last mission. I gulped nervously, fighting the panic rising within me. We'd come back to rebel headquarters.

Chapter Twenty-One

"You ready for this?" Wes asked as he took me lightly by the elbow and helped me to my feet. We hobbled down the stairs onto the platform and looked around. The entire station was completely deserted, not a soul in sight.

"I don't know," I replied. "I'm ready to be done being sick, but what exactly are we going to do to Capell?"

"Our contacts from within told us there's been unrest for a while. Lots of people think she's not really doing anything to win the war, and they're tired of hiding like rats in holes waiting for the next bomb to hit."

"I don't blame them," I grumbled in reply, remembering my very unpleasant stay in the cliffside tunnels. "So we're just going to march in there and court-marshal her?"

"Her second-in-command is a double agent. He's ready and waiting, and he's going to help. Besides, you're our best witness. We have some others waiting there that will testify against her. Trent came back up a few days ago. They moved him from the holding place in the city. He'll be given a prison sentence instead of a death sentence for offering to testify. Some of the others came up last night."

I nodded, my knees feeling trembly. The thought of seeing Terrence again scared me. I didn't know how he would react, or what would happen when him and Capell were in the same room. I let Wes hold my arm all the way across the station, out through the fence, across the parking lot and into a small shack that probably used to be used for tickets.

"Our ride should be here soon," he said. "Ah, there he is."

Wes pointed out a sleek, strangely silvery-looking vehicle sliding silently into the gap next to the booth. The window rolled down.

"Show yourself," came a gruff voice from within the car.

We left the shack. Wes bent down and pulled out his necklace, the one with the symbol of the rebellion on it. The man nodded and pushed the button to open the automatic doors.

"Get in. Things are getting...interesting."

We climbed in. Our driver sat rigid in his seat as if he had metal instead of bones in his body. His lips pursed tightly, and he remained silent the entire ride back to headquarters.

"What's with the car?" I asked.

"It's painted with the same reflective material as they use with the Invisijets," Wes whispered, his eyes darting warily about our surroundings. "It's to disguise them from the bombers, though that's not much of a worry anymore. From above, they blend into the dirt, making them nearly impossible to see."

My eyebrows twitched in confusion. "How do you know all this?"

"We drove them to Epirus."

"Are you kidding me?" I hissed. The driver's eyes flicked back towards us briefly.

"What? Isn't that how you reached the city?"

I stared at him. "We walked."

Wes's eyes grew so large I worried they'd pop out of his head. "They made you *walk*? It's a six-hundred mile trip!"

I nodded. "As far as we were told, that was the only way. We had to be stealthy, but these cars sure would have made a difference."

Wes gave a low whistle and shook his head. His eyes met mine and held them, the way they used to. I found it hard to look at him, so I shifted my gaze to my lap. Wes gently reached out and clasped his hand over mine. A wave of chills passed over my body and for a moment, I forgot about all my pain and exhaustion. Maybe he could forgive me after all. Someday.

"I'm sorry, Lily," he murmured. "I guess you were right about Capell."

Feeling slightly bolstered, I looked at him and smiled, grateful for the validation. A small, slight smile lifted his lips.

The car gradually descended the huge cliffs and parked in a small, deserted cove. Our driver got out and began checking the car over, presumably to make sure no mud or anything had kicked up onto it to give it away. Wes led me to an entrance into the tunnels I never knew about, a small, disguised door that led to about a thousand stairs.

"This is the fastest way in," Wes panted, sweat beading his brow. "Can you make it?"

I shrugged. "I kind of have to, don't I?"

"I'll help you." He slipped an arm around my waist. My skin tingled at the touch. He helped me up the stairs, one by one, around each narrow corner until we arrived at the top at last, clutching our sides and gasping for air.

"Plug your ears," Wes mumbled. He pushed the door open and immediately the loudest alarm I've ever heard went off right in our ears. I collapsed, holding my head to try to stop the throbbing. Wes gently pulled me to my feet, making sure I kept my hands over my ears, and led me through a couple dark hallways to the main meeting room. I'd never even known these tunnels existed until now. He'd probably been given privileged information when he went on his assignment. Capell always had liked him better than me. The fact glared even more obviously now knowing he'd been given a car to accomplish his mission.

She stood there when we arrived, her sinewy arms crossed over her narrow chest, her eyes mere slits in the angry redness of her face.

"What is *she* doing here?"

She turned to face someone behind her. I gasped. Terrence sat on the bottom row of the small amphitheater, still in cuffs, his eyes full of terror. "Why didn't you follow orders?"

"He tried, Capell, but we stopped him." I swear my heart stopped beating when I heard the voice. Levi. How had he gotten here so fast? I remembered suddenly that Wes had said some of the others came up here last night. Levi must have gone with them.

He stepped from the shadows, somehow looking more menacing than I'd ever thought possible. His massive shoulders bulged from beneath a tight tank top, revealing a tattoo of the symbol of Illyria, the same one that adorned our identification necklaces.

"Your orders are corrupt," said a new voice. Amelia. She stepped up next to Levi.

"You've endangered the lives of many rebels. You fraternized with the enemy and promised him not a way to win the war, but a way for him to get what he wants and possibly build a better, stronger army to kill us with. You are hereby ordered to resign for treason. It has become clear to us that you no longer have the rebellions' best interests at heart."

Capell turned to look from Wes and I on one side to Amelia and Levi on the other so fast that I thought her head might fall off.

"You can't force me to resign!" she hissed. "I alone began the rebellion! I alone devised a plan to ensure success, to stop to the fighting and the bombing! One life," she pointed to me, "is worth losing if it means saving everyone else from a bloody war!"

"I believe several of us began the rebellion, long before you took over, while you were still sipping cocktails with that scum from the south," said a deep, booming voice across the room. I followed the voice to a man with rich brown skin and deep, dark eyes. He stared at Capell with a look as hard as steel. "You knew he would have used the girl to his advantage before having her executed. You knew he would have used her DNA to create an army. You're done. Step down or we will be reduced to force."

"He already had the cure!" she shrieked. "We knew that! All he wanted was her head! It was the only way!"

"No," said the man. "What Trent developed was a first run. It cured the symptoms, and altered the Akrium sequence in the DNA until it was no longer fatal, but it did not make the infected beasts as strong or agile or capable as Miss Mitchell here. You knew what you were doing. Now *step down.*" His voice had lowered dangerously, his eyes narrowed, his jaw set.

Capell stepped back a few paces, looking like a wild animal trapped in a cage. She suddenly drew a gun from her waistband where it had been cleverly concealed, not being much larger than a slice of bread. She pointed it at me.

"*She* is the problem! Don't you see that? If it weren't for her, this war never would have started!"

"Hey!" I shouted, not thinking, not registering that she had a gun pointed at me and could take away my life at any moment. "It was *not* my choice! My DNA was able to withstand the Akrium because it wasn't a first-hand injection. I inherited its gifts from my father, who had been injected. It's not my fault I was targeted just for being alive, for being an anomaly! And for your information, the government killed my father!"

The words caught in my throat when I saw a silent figure creeping up behind Capell. Mom.

A strange, gurgling sound issued from my throat. I wanted to warn her, but I didn't want to alert Capell to her presence. She held something heavy, some kind of tool, and the look in her eyes was one of a lion about to maul some unfortunate zebra.

Everything happened so fast, but when I look back on it, things seemed to slow down right in that moment so that I caught every detail.

"Not my daughter!" mom screamed. She brought the weapon down and clubbed Capell on the head. The gun clattered to the floor, along with mom's weapon, which I now saw was a large wrench. Shouting broke out everywhere. The tall man who'd spoken out against Capell swept my mother into his arms and carried her away.

"Mom!" I finally gasped. Wes grabbed my hand and we plunged into the madness, elbowing people aside left and right, swimming through the crowds to try to find her. We finally made it through the masses of people to a door that led down some hallways I'd never seen. They were probably some kind of administration rooms or something. The man and mom were nowhere in sight.

Wes led me down one of the hallways.

"You think he's in on it?" Wes asked, his breath coming in short puffs as we ran and looked through the doorways of each room.

"No," I replied, "I think he's trying to protect her." Something about the man made it instantly clear that he was a good, humble person. I didn't know how, but somehow I knew he wouldn't hurt her.

We stumbled through corridor after corridor, looking through door after door with no sign of them. At last, we turned a corner that led to the hospital wing, one of the only areas in the vast complex I remembered.

Wes and I looked at each other.

"Hospital wing," we said at the same time, knowing without a doubt that was where she'd been taken. There was no safer place to be than with Doc Evan.

We rushed in and found mom sitting in one of the waiting chairs, asking anxious questions and refusing the tea some nurses tried to give her. The man was there as well, looking at a communicator and frowning. Evan wasn't there.

"Mom!" I cried. She looked round and was out of her seat in a flash. She wrapped her arms tightly around me, practically crushing my ribs.

"It's all right," I gasped. I realized then what she'd probably been through it since I left, worrying about what might have happened, especially with my having been gone so long. And to top it all off, she'd just watched me being held at gunpoint. I couldn't blame her for what she'd done. If Capell threatened my mother like that with a gun, I'd have probably throttled her until she cried and begged for mercy.

Mom finally pulled away, her face red and streaked with tears. "They told me you'd died on the mission, that you'd been captured by Vic…"

She broke off, sobbing. I hugged her again and looked questioningly at the man who'd carried her away.

"I'm sorry," he said in his rich baritone voice. When he wasn't angry and thundering at Capell, his voice was actually very soothing. I felt my frazzled nerves calm immediately. He stood very tall, probably at least six four, with a strong torso and powerful limbs. Again I thought about how you could tell, just looking at him, that he was good through and through.

"I didn't want your mother to get hurt. She's been through a lot in the last few weeks."

"It's okay. Thank you," I replied. "I'm glad you got to her before the crowd did."

He smiled, showing a row of perfect white teeth. The crinkles around his forehead and eyes made it clear that he was older, probably in his forties or fifties, but he must have been a very handsome young man.

"I've been looking out for her. She's a good person."

Mom had settled down a bit, so we all sat down in the chairs.

"What's your name?" I asked the man, taking the tea he offered as the nurses left and giving mom the cup she originally refused. She took it this time and sipped it quietly. It bothered me how tired and frail she seemed.

"George Windell," he replied, taking a sip from his own cup. "I imagine you have a few questions about what's been going on around here."

I nodded. The tea tasted wonderful, like mint and chamomile and heather and all sorts of other flavors mixed into one.

"Well, a week or two after you left, Capell started acting strange. Stranger than usual, I mean. She claimed that she heard you'd been abducted and killed by Vic, but we all knew something was off. She didn't send out anyone to search for your party. Your mom got herself in a state over it, understandably. We knew something was odd, something wasn't right. We got in contact with some associates down south, rebels of the rebels, I suppose, and they said they'd been in contact with your party. They explained what Terrence had done."

- 111 -

So that was who all those late night hushed interviews were with on the communicators! Eli could have told us what was going on, I thought grumpily to myself. If I'd known what they'd said and done to mom, I'd have been up north like a bat out of hell.

"That explains a lot." I gestured to myself. "I'm quite sick, as you can see. I guess that's why they didn't let me in on any of this. I haven't been feeling well enough to really do anything except sleep."

George nodded. "That's our next order of business. The others will take care of Capell. In the meantime, let's get you to Trent."

Chapter Twenty-Two

We stood up, and suddenly I felt weak.

"Can we get some food first? We've been traveling all day and haven't had very much to eat."

"Oh!" said George. "Yes, of course, I'm so sorry. I wasn't thinking. Kitchens first, then the lab."

I grimaced slightly at the word "lab." I'd never felt like so much of a freak as I did now.

All of us, mom included, followed George to the kitchen where a meal of warm bread, mashed potatoes, green beans and a small slice of beef was served. I ate ravenously, not caring that I looked like a pig as I asked for seconds.

Mom picked at her food, eating tiny bites here and there. I stopped my scarfing and reached for her hand. She looked up at me, tears welling in her eyes.

"I'm sorry, mom. I never should have left," I whispered. "But it's ok. I'm here. And we're going to make things right."

She nodded, but it didn't make any difference. She still picked at her food. Knots of worry formed in my stomach, pushing the food around and making me queasy. It felt very unsettling, trying to comfort her as if she were the child and I were the parent.

Mom looked really tired, so I took her to our little room and let her lay down. She fell asleep almost immediately. I looked at George, who must have sensed my alarm because he put his hand on my shoulder.

"She's going through some pretty severe depression, maybe even denial. She probably thinks it's a dream and she'll wake up to find that you're really gone."

"Well...I guess that makes sense," I said, my heart aching for her. "Are you a psychologist or something?"

I realized when I said it that it might have sounded rude, but he didn't seem bothered. "I used to be, before the war. I was close to retirement anyway, so I shifted my focus to fighting with the rebels."

"Will she be okay?" I asked, my voice trembling.

"Give her time. When she realizes that you're alive and not going anywhere, I think she'll be all right. Sleep is the best thing for now."

I wiped my eyes. "I'll be there when she wakes up. I mean, after my freak treatment, of course."

"I think she'll like that."

Without really knowing or caring why, I gave George a hug. He stiffened with surprise at first, then wrapped me in his arms and held me for a moment, making me feel safer than I had in a long, long time.

The lab lay situated in a back corner of the complex. Several sections were curtained off, making it clear that the lab had been hastily constructed with the arrival of the scientists. Trent approached us, relief etched on his tired face.

"Avery and I heard the worst," he whispered. "We're so glad you're safe."

Avery appeared suddenly behind him. "Lily! Should have known Capell was full of it. You don't take crap from anybody."

She punched me on the arm in her usual brusque fashion, then grinned. I smiled a little, remembering our crazy forest adventure. Somehow it felt like centuries ago, instead of just a few months.

Trent had already assembled a syringe. "This will take away the Akrium poisoning and get you back to normal," he explained.

I nodded and winced as he injected the needle into my arm. The liquid felt oddly light, as if bubbles were flowing through my bloodstream. The effect spread from my arm to my shoulder, over my chest and down into my torso and legs, giving me a feeling of jumping into a cold pool after a long day in the sun. A sigh of relief escaped me.

"Feeling good?" Trent smiled at me.

"Yeah," I mumbled, feeling heavy and tired all of a sudden.

"I put some painkiller in it as well to ease the symptoms immediately. You should be right as rain after a couple of days."

"Thanks, Trent," I replied. "I'm glad you were here."

"No problem. It's all thanks to you. Imagine feeling that kind of relief after several years."

Sympathy welled within me, along with sadness. This must have been what dad had felt like before he died, only he'd had to endure the madness that accompanied the pain towards the end. I stood up and swayed a little before Wes reached out a hand to steady me.

"The effects of the medicine are difficult to deal with until all the Akrium has been altered in your system," he said. "Until then, take it easy."

"Okay," I agreed, thinking of mom and wanting to be there for her. As I hobbled towards the door, though, a sudden thought struck me.

"Trent!" I called. He'd already rushed back to his work, but he turned and came back.

"I wanted to know…Wes said something about your first vaccine not working like this latest one. What happened to the scientists who stayed with Vic?"

Trent smiled.

"For once, I was happy to make a mistake," he replied. "The properties we stripped from the heather cleanses the body of the Akrium poisoning, while the perfected genes we found in your body replace the genes damaged by Akrium. I was so worried about a cure that I didn't think to add the strength element. In short, the first cure completely erased the Akrium from everyone's system and restored them to normal health. It takes a while, but those people will eventually return to normal. The second one restores and adds strength. The scientists with Vic will be regular people without any extraordinary abilities now that they've injected themselves with the cure. I'm sure Vic has already had a fit about that one."

I smiled at the thought.

"How did you change the second formula?" I asked, feeling curious and enthralled.

"In the first trials, all our concentration was on just fixing the damage. We inadvertently left off the genetic coding that derived the strength and stamina properties from the Akrium. So we put them back in."

I paused. "So…you've figured out how to build a superhero."

He smirked. "Something like that. But we couldn't have done it without you. No wonder Vic was desperate to get hold of you."

I marveled at the sheer magnitude of it all. I'd felt a little uneasy when Trent wanted to extract my DNA, but now, thanks to my genes, we had the upper hand.

Part of me felt a hint of pride, but I mostly felt vulnerable. What lengths would Vic go to now to get to me? Something else at the back of my mind bothered me, refusing to leave me alone, like a pesky fly buzzing around my head. I looked at Trent again and it hit me. He turned back to his work, but I reached out and tugged his arm.

"What was I injected with?" I asked. Trent's face twisted into an uncomfortable expression.

"I hope you know, Lily, I didn't ever give that creep anything," he insisted, his face growing pale. "Capell said she had some routine inspection of the lab or something and I think she stole…"

I held up a hand and cut him off. "Trent, it's fine, I know you didn't do that. I'm just curious why you made it in the first place."

A small grin played across his face. "That's our secret weapon. I've worked with the raw Akrium and figured out how to strip it of its good properties, the ones that add extra strength and sustenance to the body. The formula contains only the destructive properties, making it faster at destroying the body."

My mind reeled as the information slowly sunk in. No wonder I'd been so sick! I realized then that my natural genes made the deterioration work more slowly, but even then, if I hadn't gotten to Trent when I had, I would have started to go bald and yellow and, eventually, crazy.

"I'm working to turn it into a gas that can be dispersed over a widespread area," he continued, oblivious to the turmoil I felt. "It's our only hope for winning the war, though it might be tricky. They still have the first formula for cleansing the poisoning from the Akrium. Vic still has scientists that are loyal to his vision of a grand empire that dominates anyone in its path. They'll have been working the last month to replicate as much of that original formula as they can."

I nodded mutely, my brain feeling stretched with all the new information. I was torn between gratitude that we had such a weapon on our hands, and fear of what it could do.

"Thanks Trent," I said, shaking myself from my thoughts. "I'm sorry for keeping you from your work."

"No problem," he replied, putting a hand on my shoulder. "Just come back if you feel any adverse effects, ok?"

I nodded again and started down the hall out of the lab, feeling heavier by the minute. My thought processes began to slow. The painkiller had probably kicked in.

"Can you take me to my room?" I asked Wes, who had stayed silently by my side the whole time. I desperately wanted to talk to him, to beg his forgiveness again, but my brain was so muddied I could hardly move.

"Yeah," he finally replied, clearly battling with himself whether or not to help the traitor of his feelings. He took my arm and gently led me down the numerous corridors before I found my small room. Mom still lay on the small mattress next to mine, breathing deeply and evenly. Wes helped me onto the mattress as my vision started to darken. His hand touched my cheek briefly as my eyes closed. I tried to reach out for him, to grasp his hand, to have something to hold onto, but the blackness took my mind before I could ask him if he still loved me.

Chapter Twenty-Three

I woke suddenly, the room pitch black. It always got that way in the dead of night, without any windows in the solid rock to bring the light in. I sat up stiffly, wondering vaguely how long I'd slept as I switched on the small, battery-operated light. Mom still lay sleeping on her side, her breath coming evenly, blowing stray strands of brown hair away from her face. I noticed with dismay they were liberally streaked with gray.

With nothing to do but wait for everyone to wake up, I sat back against the wall and hugged my knees to my chest. A painful longing swept through me to see Wes. Tears came suddenly, unbidden, making my throat burn. I watched mom sleep as the tears poured freely down my face, wishing she'd wake up so I could tell her everything.

Finally, I couldn't take it anymore. I slipped to my feet, still in my clothes, and jammed my sneakers on without bothering with the laces. I crept to the door and eased it open, looking back to make sure mom still slept.

My body ached as I walked stiffly down the corridor. From what I remembered, it had been late afternoon, or possibly evening, when we'd arrived back at rebel headquarters. Though I had no idea what time it was, it had to be close to sunrise. My stomach rumbled, hungry again, so I wandered aimlessly to the kitchens, figuring I might as well pick up something for mom when she woke. My steps quickened as I thought of her, remembering my promise to be there when she got up.

The kitchens were deserted, quiet and a little eerie. I nervously crept around, grabbing some bread rolls, bottled water and dried fruit leather from the cupboards. As I bundled everything into a rough burlap bag, a sudden noise made me instinctively duck for cover. Holding my breath, I crouched behind the large counter and listened so hard my ears burned.

Nothing.

I slowly let out my breath. I'd just imagined it after all.

I stood up, clutched my sack and took a tentative step before I heard it again. Ducking down, I made a concerted effort to stay as still as possible. Footsteps. Faint, but there. Heading directly into the kitchen.

My eyes darted around, searching frantically for a better hiding spot. The vast kitchens offered nothing, being composed mostly of small cupboards and tall countertops. I found a corner in the wall and squeezed myself into it as best I could, hoping and praying that whoever it was wouldn't look this way.

The footsteps came closer. They turned into the door and paused. More walking, but slowly this time. Prowling. Checking. I clenched my teeth so hard they hurt.

My heart pounded in my ears as the steps rounded the corner of the counter, inches away from my crappy hiding spot. I buried my head in my knees, tucking my hands away and wishing I could vanish.

"Lily?"

A deep, sobbing breath escaped me as I looked up. Wes stood over me, flashlight in hand, his head cocked at an angle, asking the question that hung in the air.

"Wes..." I breathed, feeling my heart slowly return to a normal pattern of beats.

He crouched next to me, his eyes worried about and wary of me at the same time.

I cleared my throat and tried not to look like a terrified animal. "Um...I was hungry."

A small smile played across his lips. He sat on the floor, Indian style, and studied me. I looked down at my knees, still hugged to my chest, feeling distinctly uncomfortable.

"Is your mom still asleep?"

"Yeah." He set the flashlight between us at an angle so we could see each other. "I was just headed back. I wanted to get her some breakfast."

"It's two in the morning," he replied, his grin growing wider.

"It is?"

I paused, considering how off my inner clock was.

"Yep." He picked at a non-existent spot on his jeans. "No wonder you're hungry. You've been asleep since midnight last night."

I gaped at him. "But that's almost…"

"Twenty-six hours. Yeah."

I lowered my knees and looked at him. "How come you're up?"

His eyes lowered, his expression became guarded and wary again.

"Couldn't sleep."

A sudden longing to reach out and wrap myself in his arms took hold of me as I looked at him. I pulled my knees up again, not knowing what to say or do. He looked up at me, a deep sadness in his eyes.

"Lily…"

I leaned forward, dying to hear what he had to say, but he paused, lost in thought.

"Are you always…I mean, is there always going to be a part of you that wishes you'd chosen the other guy?"

I leaned back, a little shocked, but then I considered what he was really asking. It wasn't so much about Levi, but more about trust. I'd cracked under the pressure once. He wanted to know if he could trust me not to do it again.

I took a deep breath. "I want to be honest, Wes."

His shoulders slumped, a surly scowl marring his face.

"There are a lot of things I really like about Levi. He was kind to me when we were going through things that were unimaginably scary."

Wes slumped and scowled even more, refusing now to look at me. I reached out gently and took his chin in my hands, gently lifting his eyes towards mine.

"But he's not you."

Tears slipped down my cheeks, but I didn't bother to wipe them away. His eyes softened slowly as he searched my eyes. I looked boldly back at him, feeling my heart rate increase as I moved my hand to caress his cheek. I wanted so badly to hold him, kiss him, beg him to believe me, but held back for his sake.

"You really mean that?" he whispered.

"Yeah," I replied, feeling slightly hurt that he couldn't immediately sense my desperation for forgiveness. I felt some kind of odd block in my heart, like a bridge I couldn't cross without his help. "Levi is my friend, Wes, but he's not the one who knows all about my freak past and still loves me anyway. He's not the one who stayed with me through mom's sickness. He's not the one who gave up his life savings to help me cure her. He's not the one who saw past the shy, weird girl in school and learned to love me despite everything that's wrong with me. He's not the one who took me to safety when I was so sick I felt like dying."

Wes nodded, his face still furrowed in a frown. I let my hand drop, disappointed.

"You better get back to your mom," he said quietly, his voice thick. "She'll be upset if she wakes up and you're not there."

Tears came more forcefully now, making my stomach twist until I thought I'd throw up. I wondered for the millionth time if he would ever forgive me.

I stood up and gathered my things, too upset and insecure to look him directly in the eyes again. I felt a sudden rush of anger as I thought of Levi. If it weren't for him, none of this would have happened. As I walked away, he gently caught my arm with his hand. I looked down to see him staring hard into my eyes, a bewildering expression playing across his boyish features.

"I just need time, Lily. It's kind of a hard thing to go through."

I nodded and hurried away before he could see the fresh wave of tears. I ran through the halls blindly, bumping into things, not paying attention to anything at all. My stupid choices, my rash impulsiveness had cost me all the things I held dear. I wanted desperately to flee these caves once and for all, to head north, start running and never look back.

As I stepped into mine and mom's room, the sight of her still resting peacefully brought me back to earth quicker than anything. I couldn't leave mom in this state, not knowing who or what to believe. No matter what happened now, I couldn't leave her side. I plunked the bag of food down on the floor, sat down on my bed with a sigh and waited for her to wake up.

Chapter Twenty-Four

"Lily!" gasped mom after she'd woken up and looked around groggily. "You're…you're here."

"It's me," I replied with a sad smile. My conversation with Wes still wouldn't quite leave me, so though I tried to act cheerful for her, it was hard to feel it. "And I'm not going anywhere now."

I moved over to sit on the bed with her, handing her some food from the bag. She looked pale, despite the fact that she'd been out for quite a while. With an uncertain glance at me, she began wolfing down the food.

"Eat as much as you want, mom," I offered. "I already ate."

Hunger had gotten the best of me around five in the morning, so I went ahead and ate some of the provisions. Mom had finally woken around seven-thirty, making me feel a little hungry again, but I wanted her to have her fill.

Mom slowed down after a while and tipped some water from a canteen into her mouth. She put it down and stared at me long and hard.

"I want to know what's going on here. I was told you were dead, and here you are!"

I took a deep breath.

"Capell sent us on a wild goose chase," I replied, choosing my words carefully, not wanting to alarm her. "Terrence, one of the guys in our group, betrayed us. Injected me with the poison serum Trent made. It made me weak, but some of the rebels down south found us in time. Wes got me up here and Trent already treated me."

That was one plus. Trent's formula had already made me feel so much better. The sleep had done wonders too, and I almost felt back to my normal self. Oh, except for the wide crack in my heart left by Wes.

"I always thought something was a bit off about everything," she sighed. "They just told me your party was missing, and most likely dead. Then they left, just like that, not caring that my daughter was gone. The only one who helped was George."

Her lips trembled. I grabbed her hand reassuringly, trying to help her see that I wouldn't go anywhere. If I ever got my hands on Capell, it would be a sorry day for her.

"Well, it's over now," I soothed. "She's dealt with. Speaking of, do you think she's had her trial yet?"

Mom shrugged. "Probably, but we can go see."

"Are you feeling up to it?"

Mom stood up and stretched. "Yeah. I need to get out of here a bit. I spent a lot of time in here while you were gone. Besides, I've been neglecting my work, and I should get back."

A look of guilt pulled her mouth and eyes down, making her look so frail and sad. I took her hand in mine and led her to the door.

"Don't worry about it. Everyone has probably left their work to go see the burning of the witch!"

I smiled at her, hoping it looked bright and convincing. She smiled back a little, her eyes looking more alert and alive than they had before.

"Lily, I taught you better than to talk like that," she murmured, the small grin still playing across her face.

I grinned even wider. "I know. But she deserves it."

We left the room together to find the hallways abuzz with activity. One of the ladies I'd seen bustling around the complex before stopped when she saw us emerge from the room.

"Oh!" she said, her face widening into a smile. "We've been waiting for you!"

"For what?" I asked bluntly.

"We need you both to witness at the trials. Are you feeling up to it?"

I looked at mom. Her smile had been replaced with a look of grim determination.

"Yes," she said in a steely voice that didn't befit her. She looked expectantly at me.

"Um, yeah," I replied, feeling like kind of a doofus. "You mean Capell's trial?"

The woman arched her eyebrows. "Well, yes, as well as the others in your group."

I grabbed her arm involuntarily, my heart in my throat. "The others in my group?" I nearly shrieked. "The only guilty one is Terrence!"

Her eyebrows came down over her eyes. "You have to understand, Miss Mitchell, that we need to cover *all* our bases. Your group will be examined and cross-examined to determine that the others have no lurking ulterior motives."

"Any idiot can see that it was Terrence! You don't even need to talk to the others!"

She stared me down calmly. "We have our own way of doing things. If your friends are found guiltless, they will go free. The trials begin in half an hour, so I suggest you get yourselves to the amphitheater."

She walked off, her shoes tapping loudly on the linoleum that covered the floor of the hallways. My head whirled, trying to take everything in. My heart ached with worry for Levi. How could they suspect him when he'd done so much to keep me safe?

"We've got to get there," I told mom in a choked whisper. Without waiting for an answer, I took her hand and began running, my heart pounding in my ears. What would they do to him if they decided in their deluded heads that he was guilty?

"Lily, slow down!" Mom's voice slowly surfaced in the middle of all my panicked wonderings. She stopped dead in the middle of our run and turned me to look at her.

"Listen to me," she said steadily. For a moment, my heart leaped, recognizing the strong woman who'd always been my mother, shining out from her frail frame. Her eyes burned with purpose once more, the wrinkles and worry lines momentarily gone. "You still have your testimony. That's the most infallible proof they can ask. He'll be all right."

I stared at her, wondering if she could read my mind. "How…"

Mom smiled again. "I'm your mother, Lily. You don't think I can tell when you're struggling between two boys?"

I smiled sheepishly. "Is it that obvious?"

She gently brushed a stray strand of hair behind my ear.

"Yes," she replied with a smile. "But it's up to you, honey. You need to decide who you really want to be with, because it's not fair to string the other along."

She turned and continued down the hall, leaving me stunned by her words. Mom had never once shouted at me or scolded me while I was growing up. She had a way of saying things without the heat of passion, without letting emotions rule her head. And she knew how to make a person think, unlike me. I must have inherited my rashness, my impulsiveness from my father. He must have deeply loved her for her ability to calmly assess things and offer wisdom instead of advice. I felt a sudden rush of gratitude that mom was here, alive, with me. Despite all the pain I'd been through the last few months and all the trouble with Vic and this stupid war, it had been worth it to save such an amazing person as her.

My thoughts turned to Levi and Wes. I was truly worried about Levi, scared that he'd give up after all he'd been through and hand himself over without any fight. I thought of Wes, how he'd always been there, always cared for me, and knew I could never let him go. I cared for Levi, but not the way I loved Wes.

Mom was right. I still had my own testimony of the things that had happened in the woods. I alone could tell them what Levi had done and been through, since we'd been alone some of the time. I could at least return his gift of returning me to Wes by defending his honor.

With a fresh sense of determination, I followed mom to the amphitheater, where buckets of fresh fruit and bottles of water had been provided. Both of us grabbed some and took our seats.

Some people that I didn't know eventually shuffled in and took seats at the front. A chair sat on a pedestal at the bottom of the amphitheater's stooped seats, presumably for people being questioned. My eyes scanned the crowd, and I noted with surprise the presence of Eli and his rag-tag band of men. My heart leaped as Wes shuffled in and found a seat a few rows down from us, followed by strangers, presumably the allies he'd gathered from Epirus. My heart dropped, wondering if he'd seen mom and I and purposely chose to sit somewhere else.

I turned my attention to the front, trying to ignore the burning behind my eyes. I needed my wits about me. A burly man in some kind of military uniform came in, followed by a string of people in dingy green jumpsuits, hands cuffed. Levi stood among them, his lips set in a firm line and his jaw clenched. Amelia came after him. I nearly stood up and forced my way to the front, but I held my ground. They had no right to chain her, none at all. I clenched and unclenched my fists slowly. Mom put her hand gently between my shoulder blades to steady me. Terrence came behind, looking like a dog with his tail between his legs. His pale, scared face began to sweat as his bright blue eyes scanned the room. Lastly, Capell and her closest advisor, a tall man with jet-black hair and eyes came into the room, both looking venomous.

The accused took their seats at the front of the room, while George came in and stood in front of the line of people.

I did a double take, not wanting to believe what I saw. George? In charge of this *insanity*? I swallowed a huge lump in my throat, weighing the odds. If George were in charge, then this had to be just a formality. No one that kind would charge innocents. I took a deep breath and steadied myself for what was to come.

"We, the entire rebellion, except for our brothers and sisters planted in the Mainframe, are gathered to address the issue of the following accused in a plot to ally with our common enemy…"

His words faded to background noise as I looked down at the line of prisoners. Levi stared at the floor. Almost as if he felt my eyes on him, he looked up directly into my face. Instantly, the hard line of his jaw softened. He stared for an interminable amount of time. Though I wanted to, I couldn't look away. After a while, he stared back down at the floor, leaving my heart in pieces. So much for my fresh determination.

Chapter Twenty-Five

"Lily Mitchell, do you swear to tell the whole truth, to give an honest account of the events as they transpired from your view and to not withhold any information on the basis of personal feeling or aspiration?"

"I do," I replied, looking nervously at the guard before me who stared me down.

"Be seated, please," said George softly from his raised seat to the side. I sat down in the chair on the pedestal before the entire rebellion, feeling very self-conscious.

"Miss Mitchell, you have to understand that from our point of view, we know virtually nothing regarding the events that led to your near capture. For this reason, we must interrogate your entire party to ensure exactly who has conspired to bring down the rebellion by submitting to the wishes of one, Victor Hansen. Do I make myself clear?"

George spoke softly, not at all the way someone in a position of authority would normally speak. I nodded, my heart's frantic pace slowing slightly.

"Miss Mitchell, can you give us your version of events the day the fire threatened your group?"

I paused, trying to remember. "I woke up to see that a fire was coming. I don't know what caused it, but Lieutenant Allen helped me to safety. We decided to split up and look for the others since they weren't around. I found Amelia and helped her to safety. Lieutenant Allen found Havermill and we managed to outrun the flames."

George made a few notes on a notepad, his forehead wrinkled with concentration.

"What happened on the night in question that you realized you were poisoned?"

I cleared my throat. "I didn't realize it until way after the fact, but I remember that Lieutenant Allen and Amelia were already asleep while I stayed awake thinking. I don't know about Havermill, but the days following I started to get really sick. I'm sorry, I don't know much more than that except that he must have done it while I slept."

I paused for a moment, straining my memories. I suddenly recalled the stinging sensation I'd felt that night, thinking it was part of a dream.

"Um…"

George looked up from his notepad. "Yes?"

"I remember feeling something like a bee sting and my neck felt sore in the morning. I had thought it was a bad dream."

"When did Mr. Havermill confess to administering the poison?"

"Shortly after we met up with Eli's crew. There were several witnesses."

George smiled a little. "We know that, Miss Mitchell, but thank you for submitting that for the court. Who helped get you to safety?"

"Once we got to the city we had to split up," I replied, trying to choose my words carefully. I didn't want to hurt Wes more than I already had, but I didn't want to diminish what Levi had done for me either.

"Lieutenant Allen remained my guide through the city and ensured that I got to the safe house on the beach."

I glanced at Wes, almost against my will, to see his mouth had turned down into a frown. A sudden urge to stand up and shout that I was only trying to keep him from punishment seized me, but I kept still. Wes would know sooner or later. I would prove that I still cared about him.

"Did any of your party exhibit suspicious behavior?"

"No. Just Mr. Havermill."

"Thank you, Miss Mitchell, you may step off the stand."

I breathed a sigh of relief, grateful that the questioning didn't take as long as I'd thought it would. I moved into the crowd and sat next to mom. She squeezed my arm and smiled at me. For the next hour and a half, all the members of our party were interviewed. Levi kept a grimace on his face the entire time, answering questions in short two or three word sentences. It didn't take much to see that he wasn't happy. I couldn't blame him. The questioning seemed to go well, and George seemed satisfied as he called the others. Amelia, too, passed with flying colors, then Terrence took the stand.

"Terrence Havermill, you stand accused of consorting with a known traitor to the rebel cause, for knowingly injuring a fellow rebel on orders that were not cleared with the entire counsel. How do you plead?"

Terrence's chin wobbled, making him look about three years old. Suddenly I felt pity for him. I couldn't deny that what he'd done was terrible, especially holding Levi and I at gunpoint, but I couldn't help feeling bad for him.

Terrence whispered something unintelligible.

"Louder for the record, please, Mr. Havermill." George glared at him sternly.

"Guilty," he stated a little more audibly.

"Then we will rest at that. Your declaration and the testimonies of the other witnesses have confirmed your guilt. We will re-convene in a days' time to determine your sentence."

I let out the breath I didn't know I'd been holding. George suddenly rose in stature in my mind. I felt relieved to know that he wasn't going to be cruel. Terrence stepped off the stand, his legs shaking and his forehead covered with a film of sweat.

"And finally, Delaney Capell, please take the stand."

Capell looked nothing like Terrence had as she took the stand. She marched boldly up to the pedestal, took her seat and placed her cuffed hands on her crossed legs. She stared defiantly up at George, daring him to ask her questions. A bad taste tainted my mouth at the sight of her.

"Miss Capell, the charges are numerous, but let's stick to your most heinous crimes." He eyed her critically from his seat. "Miss Capell, you stand accused of manipulating your position as leader of the rebellion to join in league with our common enemy. You also stand accused of making a deal with Victor Hansen, self-proclaimed head of the Mainframe, to deliver one, Lily Mitchell, into his hands for testing which would allow him the upper hand in the war. You also stand accused of administering poison, through Mr. Havermill, to Miss Mitchell. How do you plead?"

"Guilty of all charges," she replied defiantly. She turned to the crowd, her eyes scanning until they rested on me. They narrowed viciously until they'd become mere glints in her hardened mask of a face.

"Miss Mitchell has caused this problem, not me. I was simply trying to correct the problem and alleviate the burden upon us. She is the reason we are being bombed day and night. When I spoke with Mr. Hansen, he assured me he would pull all military pursuits away from the north as soon as I delivered *her*."

George leaned forward, looking like a lion ready for the kill.

"What you fail to realize, Miss Capell, is that Victor would then have the ultimate weapon he needed to destroy us. Not only that, but his desperation for supplies and food would have caused him to annihilate the Epirians as well. You've seen how he operates in the past. What on earth made you think he would keep his end of the promise?"

Several outraged cries rose at his words. People were standing now, faces red, screaming insults at Capell, looking capable of murder. Others sat looking confused and disappointed. I wanted to join them, but felt subdued somehow. The rebellion had been weak before. How could it ever survive if constant hatred and anger were always simmering between people under the surface?

Capell's face remained cool and composed, looking almost smug. Something struck me as odd. Terrence had been terrified. Capell looked almost bored. No, not quite bored. She seemed…expectant. But expectant of what?

"Mom," I whispered. "Something isn't right."

She nodded distractedly, her forehead furrowed, her eyes narrowed in concentration.

Capell shouldn't be that cocky, I thought, panic beginning to rise. Something was very wrong.

Capell turned to George, tearing her face away from me at last.

"I know which side will win. And that is the side with whom I've allied," she said simply.

Without warning, a deafening blast echoed through the halls, making everyone scream and duck. I pulled mom down, fearful of another explosion. I tensed, waiting, watching dust and small particles of debris fall from the ceiling. When nothing happened for several seconds, I chanced a glance over the seats in front of me. Some people were stampeding for the exits, others huddled on the floor, terrified. Terrence lay sprawled across the floor near the questioning seat, which I saw, to my alarm, now stood empty. George had stood up from his podium, gun raised, looking confused and angry.

Several scientists, Trent at the lead, streamed into the amphitheater, each one loaded down with several tubes, bags and equipment.

"There's been an explosion in the lab! There's a hole in the ceiling!" cried Trent. I noticed with alarm that half his face was bloody. "Something's gone wrong, we've got to evacuate!"

Chapter Twenty-Six

I'd no more than registered what Trent had said before someone yanked my hand and pulled me through the crowd. Frantically, I scrambled for mom's hand and felt my hand close around her cold fingers. I turned around, expecting to see Wes, but got the shock of my life instead. Levi had me by the hand, his close-shaved head bobbing quickly through the crowd.

George and some of the other leaders were busy herding people towards the emergency exits through the lowest door on the cliff wall and the highest at the cliff top. Crying, frantic calls and angry mutters swirled around me in a cacophony of noise. I felt numb, lost, detached. We should have been safe here, but now nowhere was safe. My heart pounded at the thought of Wes. Where could he have gone? Had he forgotten about me? I even felt a twinge of worry for Avery and Trent. Doc, too. They'd become extensions of our little family, though I didn't notice or realize it until now.

"Levi, we've got to stop somewhere!" I cried over the panic.

He looked back, his eyes a mixture of anger, pain and fear. "We can't. We've got to get to level ground."

"But..."

Another explosion suddenly rocked the complex, feeling much closer this time. Scientists scrambled for exits everywhere, lugging heavy equipment and boxes of solutions and formulas.

"See?" he called, pulling me harder. I looked back to see mom struggling after me, her eyes wide and terrified.

We eventually filtered through the small door close to the crack in the cliff wall. We shuffled outside to the beach where I'd nearly drowned. In contrast to that day, the sky was clear and blue, almost mocking the terror of the situation. No one stuck together. The policy seemed to be every man and woman for themselves as several people scrambled up the cliffs, down the beach, anywhere but where we'd just come from.

Levi started to pull me along, but I yanked my hand away furiously and dug my heels into the sand.

"What are you doing?" he shouted. "The complex is being bombed!"

"There are people I love in there, and I'm not leaving without them!" I shouted back, my heart in my throat. "If you really care, Levi, stay with my mom until I get back with the others and don't move!"

I didn't even give him an option. I heard mom scream as I pushed against the tide of people streaming through the jagged opening in the cliff.

Eventually, I forced my way in and ducked through the swarms of rebels trying to escape. Panic started to overtake me as another explosion rattled the stone walls. I took a deep breath and shoved myself into a small recess in the wall for a moment to gather my thoughts. Instinct told me Wes was still in the amphitheater. I re-visualized the pieced-together map of the complex in my head and pushed through the wall of people to the big room down the hall.

I arrived in the amphitheater to find it nearly empty, with some deep craters in the walls. I shivered, realizing the extent of the damage and the fact that the tunnels would soon collapse under the pressure. I scanned the room frantically. The sight of a shoe, attached to a body hidden behind a chair, sent my heart into my throat. I rushed across the room, leaping across rows of seats until I reached the body. The curly brown hair, the tall lanky frame…it was Wes. His hair was matted with blood. A large chunk of the stone wall lay on the ground next to him. It looked like he'd only been grazed, but it was enough to make him bleed and knock him out. I took a deep, shuddering breath and placed my fingers gently on his neck. A faint pulse beat against my shaking fingers. He was alive.

I strained my memory, trying to recall the first aid training I'd received at school. I knew I couldn't move him, but we had to get out.

"Help!" I called frantically, hoping against hope someone would come. I stood and ran, praying that someone remained in the building. Each small room, the kitchen, the infirmary, all proved empty. My heart thudded wildly in my chest. I took in deep gulps of air, trying to calm myself down. I came at last to the labs, the rooms farthest back in the cliff tunnels. I heard voices and my heart soared. Someone might be able to help after all.

I skidded to a stop in the doorway of the lab, all my hopes plunging. Trent stood still, his hand gripping a small tube, facing Capell, who'd been freed from her bounds somehow.

"Give me the serum!" she screamed.

"You're too late, Capell," he replied evenly. "You think you've won, but you're not the only one who can plan ahead."

A few other scientists stood behind Trent, staring darkly at Capell. I noticed with satisfaction that her apparent allies had deserted her. Whoever freed her was long gone.

"Trent!" I gasped, knowing it was stupid, knowing that looking would make him vulnerable. He glanced my way, and in that split second, Capell made a lunge for the serum. Trent sidestepped just in time and she fell flat on her face. Something fell from her hand and clacked on the concrete floor. It was a tiny remote with one small, red button. Trent picked it up swiftly and placed a boot on Capell's back.

"What, Lily?" he asked tersely.

"Wes…he's unconscious. I need help to get him out."

Trent looked at me, then down at his feet. His breath lengthened and his shoulders slouched, as if pressed by some invisible burden. When he looked up again, he nodded slowly to the other two scientists with him.

"No," said one of them, a tall, muscular man with a crew cut. "We're seeing this through."

"There are more important things to think about, Johnson," Trent replied quietly. "We knew it would happen sooner or later. I know you both want to be here, but you can't. Just help Lily. Please."

The two scientists still refused to move.

"NOW!" Trent thundered, making me jump. Both the scientists looked at him in unison, seeming on the verge of tears. The one who hadn't spoken, a pale man with a shock of blond hair, came forward and took the serum that Trent offered him.

"Thanks, Robertson," said Trent, his voice strained. "It's…it's been a pleasure working with you both. Keep going with our research."

Robertson nodded, blinking furiously.

The hair on the back of my neck prickled. Something wasn't right. Huge, burly men like that didn't cry.

"Lily," said Trent slowly, "do me a favor?"

"Trent, what are you…"

"Tell Avery I'm sorry," he interrupted, a catch in his voice. "And…and that I love her. More than anything."

"What is going-"

Before I could say another word, Johnson scooped me up and carried me away from the door while Robertson followed, the small vial clutched tightly in his hand. Trent checked to make sure Capell was still pinned, then looked out at us, tears in his eyes as he lifted the remote. He pressed his thumb to the button. The scientists and I were flying now, running down the hall as if our lives depended on it.

And suddenly it hit me.

"No…" I gasped. "No, no, no!"

I flailed and pounded my fists against Johnson's back, but to no avail. He continued to run.

"NO!" screamed a shrill female voice behind me. Capell. Moments later, a shattering explosion tore through the hall, deafening us.

"Trent!" I screamed, a sob ripping from my throat.

My head spun and the room began to tilt dizzily. An odd ringing sounded in my ears.

He'd sacrificed himself to get rid of Capell. To keep her from taking the finished formula to Vic. Burning tears leaked from my eyes, searing my cheeks on their way down.

Why would he do that? Why would he make Avery a widow?

We'd reached the amphitheater before I could register what was happening. Johnson plunked me down and gripped my shoulders.

"Look at me," he instructed through tears of his own. I looked into his eyes, seeing my pain mirrored there. "We have to get out with Wes. The tunnels are all gonna go any minute, and I need you to help us. Can you do that?"

He was used to dealing with emergencies. I nodded numbly.

"Good," he said, releasing me. "Take us to Wes."

I scanned the amphitheater until I saw Wes's shoes peeking out from behind the row of chairs. I motioned the men forward. One took his pulse, nodded and gently turned him over. One man took his feet. The other gently wrapped his arms under and around Wes's torso. Somehow we scrambled to the hall and made it out of the exit. The tunnels were completely deserted as we squeezed out of the opening in the cliff. The four of us tumbled out onto the beach into the shade of the cliff side. Johnson and Robertson gently laid Wes down on the sand and started checking him head to toe. I sat numbly next to Wes, hugging my knees to my chest, trying to rid myself of the extreme pressure and pain building in my heart. I couldn't fight the tears that kept coming. I couldn't erase the memory of Trent's face in his final moments, his plea to tell Avery his dying words.

I buried my face in my arms, wishing to disappear, feeling horrible that I hadn't done more to help Trent, that I hadn't made him come with us. I felt a hand on my shoulder and looked up warily. Robertson looked at me, his brown eyes also filled with pain.

"Lily, don't blame yourself for what happened. Trent knew something like this would probably happen. We couldn't let Capell go with the formula. It would have been the end for all of us. Trent…died a hero."

I gulped, fresh tears streaming from my face.

"But we could have gotten him out," I snapped. "Blown the lab with Capell in it. We could have done *something*! We just ran away like cowards!"

He shook his head gently. "You think I'm not dying inside too? I've known Trent for years. We were both in the first group that tested the akrium. We lived in that awful cave in the forest for uncounted years. He was one of my best friends. I would have taken his place in a minute. But if he'd let her up, that would have been the end of it. Capell is stronger than she looks."

"She's not that strong," I muttered, wiping my face.

"She is, Lily. And she would have stopped at nothing. She was convinced that cooperating with Vic was the only way to win. It would have meant your death."

I shrugged away from him. I knew I was being ungrateful and cold, but I would have given my life if it meant Trent didn't have to die in such a horrible way. What would I tell Avery? How could I face her again?

A loud, crashing, crumbling sounded overhead. All of us watched silently as the tunnels began to cave in.

Chapter Twenty-Seven

"Lily, you've got to eat something."

I pushed away the small piece of bread that Levi offered me and turned away, feeling sick inside. Things had never been so awful. I just wanted to disappear.

A group of us huddled against the beach cliffs farther down from the tunnels, cold and terrified that bombers would fly over any minute. The day had passed in a haze to a dreary, drizzly night. Mom sat next to me, holding my hand comfortingly. She waved Levi away as he once more tried to persuade me to eat. He finally gave up and stomped away to sit farther down the wall.

Wes lay in the sand on my opposite side, about an arms-length from me, huddled against the cold. I'd covered him with a blanket because he still hadn't woken up. Robertson and Johnson had done a good job bandaging him up with what we had available, but he still lay unconscious. My heart raced in panic, though the bombings had long since stopped.

Wes's pulse seemed regular, but his face remained pale and covered in a cold sweat. Doc had made it out, thankfully, and said Wes had a blow to the head, but nothing he wouldn't recover from. He checked on him periodically and trickled water into his open mouth.

My eyes eventually grew itchy and heavy, so I laid my head on mom's shoulder to try to get some rest. All of us were still in severe shock. Some had gone out and searched for other survivors, bringing them back to the small stretch of beach where we encamped. About two-thirds of our group had made it out alive. So many had died, some trampled in the mad rush for the exits, some from bombings on the cliff top. Amazingly, no one besides Wes had been struck by debris in the amphitheater. I'd cried for a long time about Trent, but my body seemed empty of tears now. I couldn't possibly cry anymore, even if I'd wanted to.

There was no sign of Avery.

I tried to push these thoughts from my mind and relax at least a little bit. Mom refused to sleep, and slipped covert glances my way every now and again. A few years ago, it might have irritated me, but now I felt thankful for her watchful care. It was nice to be looked after since I'd had to look out for myself for the last few months.

"Lily?"

My eyes popped open. My heart leaped as I saw Wes sitting up and rubbing his head.

"Wes," I whispered. I looked at mom, who smiled understandingly. I noticed Levi shoot us a dark look over my mom's head. I let go of her hand gently and knelt next to Wes.

"How are you?" I asked quietly. He sat up and rubbed his eyes.

"I don't know," he replied. He smiled a little. I worried for a moment that he had amnesia or something, but he brushed the sand off of his ear and rumpled the blanket in his hands. He seemed normal enough.

"What happened?" he asked, noticing his odd surroundings for the first time.

"This girl is a hero," said a voice nearby. I looked up to see Robertson standing there with a small bit of bread and some crackers. He handed them to Wes.

"She noticed you weren't out of the complex and came looking for you. She found you and got us to help get you out."

Robertson gave a small smile, then walked back to his spot on the cliff-side. Wes watched him while my cheeks burned with embarrassment. I'd wanted to tell Wes in my own way, but this guy had just barged in and done it for me. I supposed I should have been grateful, but mostly I just felt awkward. It made me feel weird that he overheard us enough to come and tell Wes what happened.

"You really did that? For me?" Wes asked slowly, leaving his food untouched and turning his gaze to me.

A sob escaped my throat as I looked at him. How could he ask something like that? In that way, so unbelieving?

"Of course," I choked out. "Why wouldn't I?"

"I just…I thought that when you told me you kissed that other guy that I'd done something wrong, something to make you feel like I didn't love you anymore. I didn't know what to think. I figured if something happened to me, you would just be ok with it since you have him."

He twisted his hands nervously, clamping his mouth shut to keep from saying anymore.

I clasped one of his hands with mine, my heart beginning to feel light for the first time in a long time.

"I never stopped loving you, Wes," I whispered. "It didn't mean anything, and it never will. The *only* one I want to be with is you."

He stared at me for a long moment, his eyes looking deeply into mine. He touched my cheek with the tips of his fingers, and unexpectedly, his lips pressed against mine. An inexplicable wave of intensity stole over me, making my skin tingle from my scalp to my toes. An incredible feeling stole over me, as if I were a prisoner released from a long sentence. At that moment, nothing felt impossible.

He pulled back and smiled, blushing a little. We drew closer together, his fingers weaving through my hair as we kissed again, as deeply and passionately as we had that first time on the dock. I was only slightly aware that other people were watching. In that moment, I just didn't care.

I fell asleep in his arms, warm and comfortable despite the chill in the air. We woke the next day to find the others packing up what few belongings we still had. Several of them looked lost. I supposed we were just a bit lost, considering our impenetrable fortress had been annihilated.

Wes and I stood up and walked over to mom, who was busy packing supplies.

"What's going on?" I asked, still rubbing sleep from my eyes.

"We're going to try to hunt down some shelter," she replied. "We can't stay out in the open like this."

I took her hand and she paused to look up at me. She smiled at Wes, but her lips were tight with tension.

"What happened exactly?" I asked. "Who compromised us?"

Mom rolled her eyes. "Who do you think?"

"Yeah, but how would Capell have talked to Vic and the others without us knowing?"

Mom shrugged. "Something tells me she knew she was going to get caught. She somehow got wind that things went south and that Terrence didn't deliver you like he was supposed to. Anything she said to him was an act. She didn't want us getting suspicious. So, she set things up to blow at the critical moment."

I frowned. It was so like that woman to always be one step ahead. At least she wouldn't be a problem anymore. Then again, I admitted guiltily to myself, it had cost Trent his life. A bitter taste filled my mouth as I remembered him telling us to go.

"I guess it's no surprise," sighed Wes. "Have any others filtered back through the night?"

"Some." Mom gestured vaguely to the group of people packing bags. My stomach clenched as I saw Avery standing in the midst of them, her wild blond hair now flat on her skull, eyes a dull shade of what they used to be. I wondered if she knew. Though I didn't want to, I knew I had to talk to her, let her know what happened. At the very least, I could offer my condolences.

"I'll be right back," I whispered to mom and Wes. With a deep breath, I walked slowly across the sand to Avery. She looked at me as I approached, but seemed to stare right through me.

"Um…" I started, but my voice cracked right away. Tears rose in my eyes and I couldn't push them down. Avery said nothing. She just walked right up to me and put her arms around me. We hugged and cried for an interminable amount of time until I finally pulled away and held her shoulders gently.

"I'm so sorry," I sobbed. "He saved my life. I don't even know what to say. I wish it had been me that died…I wish…"

I trailed off into more sobs, wishing I could disappear, wishing she would stop staring at me, not a hint of a tear in her eye. She looked down at her feet, then back up at me.

"I knew it was coming," she replied, her voice hoarse and rough from crying. "He let me know something like this might happen, and told me to get myself out, but a part of me always hoped he would get out, that some miracle would happen."

She looked out at the ocean, a tear starting down her cheek at last.

"Seems unfair, doesn't it?" she continued. "We were finally getting back on better terms. But…we had the chance…to…to say goodbye."

She stopped talking as her hand moved to her mouth. Sobs shook her thin frame as her eyes closed painfully tight, making my heart break. Guilt burned my cheeks and my throat as I stood awkwardly, not knowing what to say or do. I suddenly remembered Trent's last request.

"He did say…" I started awkwardly, "that he was sorry and that he loves you more than anything." There. I'd managed to get the words out before I broke down again.

Avery cried some more, her shoulders shaking violently. I put my arm around her shoulders and we cried together for a long time.

"Lily," she finally said, "it's not your fault. I hope you don't feel like you killed him, or that his sacrifice was in vain. The other guys feel the same way, but I hope you know that Trent warned me this might happen. Nothing is your fault, or theirs. Please remember that."

I nodded mutely, feeling some of the pressure lift. I gave her another hug, not trusting myself to talk. Things were so confusing, awful and wonderful at the same time. We pulled apart and she gave my hand a small squeeze.

I dried my tears and looked up at her. "We may have lost everything, but it's not the end, Avery. Let's strike back," I said, a growing anger working its way into my voice. "Let's pay Vic back for everything he's done to us."

Avery's eyes blazed, and she began to look somewhat like her old self.

"I couldn't agree more."

Chapter Twenty-Eight

"How much of the developed serum do we have left?" I asked Robertson of the briskly, trying to get people moving. Those of the resistance that remained seemed lost and no longer interested in the cause.

"Trent had a cache hidden in various parts of the bunker, but it's probably all gone," he replied. "I have a pouch with me that contains some of it in liquid form, but not nearly enough for the whole Mainframe."

"Then we need to go in and search for the remainder. Some might have survived if it was hidden well enough."

He shrugged. "We can try. You'll need some gas masks, though, because of radiation."

"Fine," I replied distractedly.

Wes, Avery, Robertson, Johnson and I all donned masks and headed for the complex. Some others had gone into the complex before us to try to find food, but to no avail. With limited supplies, several of our allies had left to try to make their way in our war-torn world. The rebellion had pretty much disbanded. No one felt any hope. Capell's attack had been too well timed. I felt a surge of bitterness as I wondered why she'd even wanted to be the leader of the rebellion. As we tramped through the burned hallways, I remembered that she'd been the governor of the north prior to the war. Maybe she'd been shunted into the rebellion by the wish of the people and her position of leadership. The thought didn't make me feel any sorrier for her fate, and my own callousness over her death worried me slightly.

We followed Johnson to the lab where Trent had died. I panicked slightly as we entered the room, wondering if we'd see Trent's body, but I didn't need to worry. Everything lay coated with a fine layer of ash. Robertson opened several cupboards and riffled among the shelves, but shook his head.

"It's all burned," he said, his voice oddly distorted through the mask. "Let's check the other caches."

The process went on for hours, moving from one area of the complex to the next. Trent had been very thorough, very prepared. He'd hidden vials of the formula in several places. For the longest time, we had no luck. While searching in the amphitheater, though, we finally found something worthwhile. A case containing forty or so vials remained intact underneath the judges' podium. Near noon, we found another in Doc's office under his exam table. We combed the complex thoroughly, but only found about a hundred vials at our disposal.

As we left the complex and removed our masks, I breathed deeply of the fresh salt air. It was a relief to be away from the memories and horror of the cramped tunnels.

"So?" I asked.

Robertson shrugged. "Trent never got the chance to develop a gas form of the substance. We were working on developing it when the bombs went off. We've got more of the formula than I thought we would, but it still might not be enough for the Mainframe."

I paused, deep in thought. Different aspects of the plan had trickled down to me in the last few days, the main plan being to turn the poison formula into a gas and releasing it into the vents of the Mainframe. Our allies within already had a code word to listen for, alerting them to put on masks while the traitors within were gassed. However, the plan to get the Mainframe workers in the rebellion out and destroy the Invisijets had gone forward early with the Terrence's betrayal, so the need for the gas wasn't quite so urgent anymore.

"What if we just put the liquid into tranquilizer form and shoot the rogue scientists? If we get past them, it's just a bunch of civilians to deal with from there," Wes said suddenly. I turned to him and smiled. I hadn't thought of it, but it was brilliant.

"We could, but we need tranquilizer guns and a way to put the liquid into some bullets."

"What if we stole them?" I asked.

Johnson raised his eyebrows. "I guess we could, if you know where to get them."

Wes suddenly grinned. "No need to steal. I know someone who would be more than willing to supply us. But we need to get down south."

"To where, exactly?" asked Robertson.

"Epirus."

- 143 -

* * *

After we'd rallied what remained of our small group, including mom, Levi, Avery and the few remaining scientists, we walked to the train station in the small town near the cliffs. As we suspected, no train sat waiting for us.

"Wouldn't it be risky anyway?" asked mom. I knew she was remembering the time she'd been arrested at the train station, trying to get to me.

"It's the quickest way to get there," said Wes. "We don't have rebel cars anymore, or gas for that matter."

We'd gotten this far, and all of us felt the frustration of needing to move quick but not being able to. Walking, it would take days to get to Arduba, much less to Epirus, which was much further south than the capitol.

"Wait a minute," I said, growing excited as an idea took hold of me. "Are there any sea ports nearby?"

The others wrinkled their brows, deep in thought. One of the scientists suddenly nodded excitedly.

"Apollonia! It's not too far from here," he replied.

"Yeah, but will anyone be chartering a boat right now? Especially for what we want to do?" Levi questioned, looking skeptical. "We don't have anything to pay with. No one is going to be crazy enough to sail us to Epirus, then Arduba. It's suicide."

"We can at least try," I shot back, feeling a little annoyed.

He shrugged, and nobody had any further objections, so we headed south towards Apollonia, keeping the ocean on our right. The sun had begun to set when we finally reached what had once been a bustling seaside port. Shutters were closed on each of the small cottages that lined the streets of the town. Not a soul was in sight, but I still hoped that we'd be able to find someone who could direct us.

A few more blocks took us to a small marina, where a few boats sat stranded in the shallows like a lost family of fish. Most were sailboats, but there were a few high power speedboats. Nobody seemed to be around.

We shuffled around and knocked on doors, but no one answered. We tried the boathouse as well with no luck. The town seemed to be deserted. Perhaps they'd had a bomb threat and went underground.

I looked at Avery, who had a shadow of that mischievous glint in her eyes. The corners of my lips lifted almost of their own accord. I knew what she was thinking. When I met her all those months ago, I would have objected on the spot, but times were beyond desperate now.

"Avery can do it," I said quietly. "We'll break into the boathouse, find some keys and haul it out of here. She can drive a boat. I've seen her do it before."

Immediately, everyone started to object. Mom took it worst of all, looking at me as if I'd sprouted an extra head. I knew it had to be hard on her, watching her daughter break the law so carelessly, but was there even a law anymore? Something had to be done to stop Vic, to stop the suffering he'd caused.

"We can't just take someone's property," she pointed out. "I'm pretty sure I taught you better than that, Lily."

"You did, mom," I sighed. "I don't want to do it either, but it's our only option. You have to admit it."

Everyone argued for a while, but in the end, no one could give a good enough argument not to take a boat. Avery even offered the idea of returning it someday, which we all knew would be pretty much impossible.

We trooped over to the boathouse, smashed a window and unlocked the door. Avery went through the room quickly but only produced one set, which most likely belonged to the harbor master. She examined the keys carefully, then tried them on several boats before she got the right one. The boat was *tiny*. A two-seater at most, and there were eight of us. A small space behind the seats might fit two or three of us, and one between the seats. Some could possibly fit in the small cargo square in the back. But it would be very tight and uncomfortable.

Avery took charge. "I'll have to drive, and Elaine needs to be on the passenger seat," she directed. "Lily, why don't you squeeze between the seats so you can help me navigate. You three can squeeze behind our seats. Wes and Levi, you'll have to sit in the cargo hold."

Wes and Levi looked daggers at each other. I felt more than a little worried. The cargo hold was little more than a slight, square-shaped padded indentation on the back of the boat. They'd have to grip the edge of the pit with the seats just to keep steady. And Avery wasn't exactly a careful driver.

After scooting the seats up as far as they would go, we started putting everyone into their various places. It took some maneuvering, but we finally crammed all eight of us into the minuscule boat. We'd found some rope in the glove compartment and lashed it across the seats so that Wes and Levi would have a little something more to hold on to. They sat as far away from each other as possible.

Avery turned the key again and revved the engine. At that moment, a red-faced pudgy man flew from one of the houses, obviously angry.

"Hold on!" I cried to Levi and Wes. "Avery, punch it!"

We zoomed away from the shore at lightning speed, leaving the screaming, fist-shaking man behind us.

Chapter Twenty-Nine

As predicted, Avery drove like a madwoman. We reached the main port in Epirus about midnight. Wearily, all of us climbed out of the small boat and stretched our cramped muscles. My eyes ached from straining them against the wind, my voice hoarse from yelling directions. Salt spray coated my hair, making it feel tacky. My legs and arms were completely numb from crouching between mom and Avery and holding on for dear life. Wes and Levi had survived, but I noticed bruises on their arms and legs from where they'd bounced with the motion of the boat.

"Not looking forward to doing that again," muttered Levi.

"Well, at least the trip back will be shorter," I replied icily.

Wes groaned and stretched. "You'd all better stay put here. I know my way around. I'll find Conley and get our supplies."

My stomach howled at me, reminding me just how long it had been since our last meal.

"Can you get us some food too?" I called after him. He just waved as he tromped off down the road. A ripple of irritation coursed through me. Hopefully, that meant yes.

"We'd better lay low," said Avery, her eyes darting around. I agreed. The last time we'd been here had been far less than pleasant, though the port wasn't nearly as busy as it had been when we'd sailed here on an Epirian ship. We'd moored the boat on a faraway dock, hoping to be inconspicuous. Without a lot of options, we hunkered down behind some shipping crates. Somewhere along the line, I fell asleep, but jolted awake when someone poked me in the arm. I looked up blearily to see Levi staring intently at me.

"What's wrong?" I asked groggily.

He shifted uncomfortably. "Um…nothing, really. I just wanted to talk."

Instantly, I was on guard. It had taken extreme trust for Wes to leave me with Levi and I wasn't about to break his trust or lose him again.

"Levi, I'm sorry," I blurted out before he could say anything. "But you're just going to have to accept that I want to be with Wes."

"That's not what I wanted to ask," he said. A scowl came over his face, making him look a little scary in the dim light.

"Well…what then?"

He took a deep breath. "I just want to know…did you feel anything for me? Even if you didn't choose me, I just want to know if you felt the same way. At any point."

That was different. I twisted my sleeves, trying to come up with what to say. Of course I'd had feelings for him. They had been real. But how could I stay loyal to Wes and not completely break Levi? How could I possibly answer that question? It didn't seem fair, and I wondered if he was trying deliberately to trap me in my words.

"Well…yeah, I did, if we're being perfectly honest," I replied carefully. "I did feel kind of abandoned when Wes came here to look for help. But he did it for me. He wants the war to end so we *can* have a life together."

"He has a funny way of showing it," Levi muttered. "Especially since he just deserted you again."

"He didn't want to put me or anyone else in danger," I shot back. "Stop pretending you know everything, and stop criticizing him."

Levi looked down, his face pale, shoulders slumped, and suddenly I felt such pity for him. He'd had a hard life too, and here I was, making it even harder.

"Look, Levi, you do mean a lot to me. I did kiss you back, and I could have had deep feelings for you if those feelings weren't already reserved for Wes. He was there for me in a time when life was so dark I didn't think I'd ever survive. I can't…I can't just throw that away."

He looked up, his face full of sorrow and resignation.

"Ok. That's all I wanted to know."

The rest of the night passed in uncomfortable silence. I leaned against a shipping crate, wide awake, completely unable to even feel tired anymore, though I knew my body was exhausted. As the sun crept slowly into the sky, Wes picked his way carefully through the cargo scattered on the deck, looking for us. A tall, somewhat narrow-looking man walked with him. They each carried a massive bundle.

"Wes!" I hissed quietly. The dock was sure to be busier during the day and I wanted to avoid being seen. Wes veered in the direction of our group and ducked down behind the crates.

"Lily, this is Conley," he said, gesturing to the man behind him. "He helped me the last time I was in Epirus, and he's willing to help us now."

Conley smiled. "So *this* is Lily."

Wes blushed slightly. I shook Conley's hand, giving Wes a look. Clearly, they'd talked about me.

"He knew about you when I came here as a soldier," Wes muttered to me. "He knew you had a price on your head and that I was trying to protect you. That's all."

I shrugged, too tired and upset about the conversation with Levi to give Wes a hard time. Conley looked at our small group, counting heads.

"We can get them all into a crawler," he said to Wes. At our confused stares, Wes informed us that crawlers were the Epirian word for rover.

"And we'll stop by the lab before we drive up, right?" Wes asked.

"Hold on, hold on," I interrupted. "So we're going to drive a massive military vehicle straight into the capitol?" I asked, shooting Conley a look. I still wasn't sure if I liked him or not. He seemed nice enough, but it was kind of his fault Wes came back to the south in the first place. Conley must have been the friend that he'd needed to apologize to.

"Well, what do you suggest?" he asked. "It is a war zone."

"Won't it make us just a little conspicuous?"

"We'll be safer in something like that," Avery chimed in. "Stealth doesn't matter anymore, Lily. We've got to get to the capitol. And fast."

"Fine." I shrugged, even more irritated that Avery was suddenly all about what Conley directed. My eyes felt gritty and heavy. I knew my fatigue was making me unreasonable, but I didn't like that a foreigner, someone who'd never even been to Illyria or seen the war there, was suddenly in charge.

"It's okay, Lily. Conley's been in the Epirian military a long time. He can lead the invasion," Wes whispered.

"Ok, it's fine, whatever," I replied. He gave me a look, then shrugged.

Conley led us carefully through the docks to a large building in some kind of town square. Behind the building were huge garages that housed the "crawlers." Conley selected the keys from a safe at the back of the room, and soon we'd all climbed into the massive vehicle. The interior was surprisingly comfortable. I settled against Wes's shoulder, noting the dark look from Levi, before I fell fast asleep.

I woke later in the crawler, feeling much better. I looked around and noticed that Wes, Conley and all the scientists were gone.

"Where'd everybody go?" I asked blearily. Mom glanced around my way, having clearly just woken up.

"You passed out before you could hear the plan," she teased, ruffling my hair lovingly. "They've still got to develop the tranquilizer bullets to fit the guns before we can head up there. The scientists are working on it in the lab right now."

"Oh." I rubbed the sleep from my eyes, vaguely remembering that Wes had mentioned something about going to a lab.

Suddenly, a loud clamor sounded from above. The circular door on the ceiling of the crawler opened and Wes, Conley and the three scientists dropped in, breathing hard.

"Go!" shouted Wes.

"What's going on?" Levi spoke up from his corner. Wes shot him a look before answering.

"Conley has lots of military clearance, but he doesn't exactly have permission for the labs. We were discovered."

A loud rumbling sounded beneath us as the engines roared to life. Conley tore out of there, running over sidewalks and scattered debris. We bumped and jolted around in our seats, barely able to hold on.

"Why is Conley so willing to help you?" I asked suddenly. "Didn't he help you get some kind of job the first time you were here too?"

Wes shrugged. "I think he felt bad for all the soldiers that came into Epirus. He knew we didn't want to fight. I tried to help some Epirians that were injured, and he figured he could trust me. He was impressed, too, that I came back to apologize. It's lucky I did," he interjected meaningfully, "because now we have a powerful ally."

I didn't reply. I knew it was probably childish, but I felt a little annoyed that he hadn't explained all this to me while we were in the rebel compound. Sure, I'd

- 150 -

kept secrets from him and kissed Levi, but there was so much he'd never told me either.

But then as I looked at him, his face softened into a smile. He reached for my hand and I took it, feeling just slightly embarrassed that mom was sitting right there.

"I know you're probably still mad at me for leaving," he said.

"Well, that's kind of saying the least of it," I replied, feeling immediately bad for being so snotty. He took it in stride.

"Lily, everything I do is for you. This war will end, life will go on. We'll finally be able to be together without being torn apart all the time. Our goal right now is to get Vic out of the way."

I squeezed his hand, realizing that I was being a bit unfair. Wes had sacrificed tremendously for me in the short time we'd known each other. And what had I done? I blushed with shame and looked down at the floor of the massive vehicle.

Wes produced some dry rations, crackers, dehydrated fruit, bottles of water and cold, canned chicken. All of us ate ravenously. My shriveled stomach protested a bit at the onslaught of all that food, but I didn't care. I ate until I felt sick.

All of us became tense as Conley tried to navigate through the massive forest on the border between our two countries, each of us expecting an attack from somewhere at some point. But miraculously, nothing happened.

"Whoa!" he cried from the front. All of us jumped to our feet, immediately alert as the massive vehicle shuddered slowly to a stop. Wes leapt up and opened the hatch. I climbed up beside him and poked my head out.

"Oh my…" he trailed off, his voice choking slightly. We'd come to the edge of Arduba, the capitol city, our *home*. It looked worse than ever, worse even than the last time I'd been here just a few days ago. Buildings lay crumbling in their own ashes, cowering before the Mainframe building atop the cliffs that overlooked the ocean. Some had been completely swept away, nothing more than a pile of unintelligible rubble. Some were still on fire, making the air ashy and unbreathable. A cloud of despair and rancor hung thickly in the cloudy, winter sky. Concrete and asphalt roads had been broken up, cracked, mutilated. Not a soul was in sight. Not a soul, except one. He stood in the middle of the devastated Front

Street, in the middle of the ten lanes. His arms were crossed over his massive barrel of a chest, eyes flashing eerily in the dim light.

"About time you showed up, girl," he sneered in that raspy, awful voice.

Chapter Thirty

"Lycus?" I gasped unbelievingly.

He smirked. "None other."

"Where's Vic?" I shot at him, anger rising in my voice. Here was the last person I wanted to see, the beast who'd turned traitor from the other scientists, the one who'd given Vic the cure. I knew now that we could win, that we had a superior formula, but the thought didn't comfort me much at that moment. Lycus had been hardened by years in the Shadowlands, years of growing his hatred towards me, the anomaly that escaped the curse of the Akrium. I recognized the look of revenge in his eyes.

"He's protecting what's left of the Mainframe. Your little rebellion did get in some good shots before we crushed them, I'll give them that."

A stab of fear shot through my heart for the others in the rebellion, but I pushed it down. I needed to have a clear head. My anger began to pulse through me, giving me the now familiar strength that made me who I am. I thought of Trent as a low growl escaped my throat.

Next to me, Wes carefully hauled up his gun. I looked at him and he nodded slightly. He'd loaded the tranquilizer bullet.

Lycus laughed. "Go ahead, boy. I have a vest on. Nothing's gonna kill me."

"We don't want to shoot," said Wes. "This is a warning. This bullet *will* kill you."

Lycus laughed again, lifting his arm to motion to someone. Literally hundreds of beasts suddenly jumped out from around and within the decimated buildings, carrying everything from machetes to crude, whittled spears.

"Where did they all come from?" I gasped, astonished at the sheer numbers. At least half of the Mainframe workers had worked secretly for the rebellion. How had they turned into this? Many of them had yellowed skin, bald or balding heads, wild eyes, all the symptoms of a beast close to death.

"They…they injected them!" Wes cried, his eyes wide.

Suddenly it hit me like a ton of bricks. Capell would have known. She knew the plan to infiltrate the Mainframe, to release the gas of the new Akrium formula, to disable all the beasts. She'd gotten word to Vic before it could happen. They must have been able to destroy the jets before Vic got to them. He must have found out who worked for the rebellion and injected them without the cure. They were doomed. They were most likely livid that we hadn't gotten here earlier.

We were too late.

I ground my teeth in fury, wishing Capell were still alive so I could make her pay for all the lives she'd destroyed. That coward had taken the easy way out, and in the process, ruined us all. Ruined the rebellion. Ruined *everything*.

Shock and anger began to turn to despair. I looked at Wes, wishing we could disappear from here. The beasts raged towards the crawler, insane, wanting revenge for taking too much time, for not getting the rebellion together. We were nine against hundreds, maybe thousands. I could just imagine Vic sitting in his massive penthouse office, smoothing his greasy hair, drinking his whiskey and smiling over everything. Knowing he'd won.

With a sudden roar of rage, I leapt from the top of the crawler. I heard Wes calling me back, his voice panicked and shrill, but the feral part of me had suddenly taken over. All these beasts probably had bulletproof vests, probably had much more protection than I did, but I didn't care. I'd had it. I heard Wes clunk down on the concrete beside me.

As I leapt onto the concrete and slammed the first beast against the metal side of the crawler, it suddenly hit me that I was an eighteen year-old girl with no extraordinary power except my hybrid freakiness. Who was I to stand against all these maniacs?

Then I remembered mom, mom who I loved dearly more than anything and who I'd spent the last few years of my life protecting. I thought of Wes, the one who'd healed my broken heart, who'd rescued me from despair, who'd given his savings to keep my mother alive. I thought of Levi, whose life had been directed by the fleeting whims of the Mainframe and the rebellion. My anger boiled like poison inside my veins, making my heart pound furiously, pumping every bit of the enhanced adrenaline through my body. I let out another roar, fully embracing the beast within me, and threw another beast into the crawler. I would get at Vic if I had to kill everyone in my path.

"Lily! Watch out!"

I looked back to see Wes motioning to me from beside the crawler, the rifle still in his hand. I looked to where he pointed and saw Lycus headed for me.

"Give me the gun!" I cried. A moment's hesitation crossed his face before he handed the gun to me, carefully guiding my hands into position on the weapon's slender body.

"It only has one bullet! That's all it can hold at a time," he explained. "Don't miss."

"Don't worry," I replied darkly. "I won't."

I turned around and strode furiously towards Lycus.

"You're not going to kill me, girl. I have a vest. We all have bulletproof vests. You're done for," he taunted. Without breaking stride, I lifted the gun to my eye, moved the crosshairs to my target and pulled the trigger. Lycus staggered as the bullet hit his leg, but he quickly gathered himself and moved towards me. His hand grasped my neck and lifted me from the ground. The gun slipped and fell from my grasp. I strained the muscles in my neck, trying not to let him squeeze the life from me. Part of me panicked, but I also had faith in the solution that Trent had given his life for. He knew what he'd been doing, and knew better than anyone how to make Akrium work the way it needed to.

"You've been nothing but trouble, girl, and now I'm going to get rid of you. Then I'm going to get rid of all your nasty little friends."

I gasped a little, but tried to stay calm. Any minute…

"Have any last words, girl? I'm sure Vic will want to hear every detail of how I killed the bane of his existence."

His putrid breath washed over me as he pulled me closer. I noticed that even with the cure, he still looked manic, his eyes still flashed. His hair hadn't grown back after the cure, and patches of his skin were still yellow. I realized, with a surge of hope, that the first cure still had a lot of kinks. Trent's formula would definitely bring Lycus down.

"Still stubborn as ever, eh?" Lycus sneered. "Well, no matter. Vic has won. I can see the despair in your eyes, and I'm sure he'll love hearing all about your death."

His fingers squeezed tighter around my throat, making stars pop before my eyes. The edges of my vision had started to blacken when Lycus suddenly gasped. A yellow sheen spread quickly over his skin. What little hair had started to grow

- 155 -

back fell out. His eyes blackened, flashing psychotically in the dim light. With the last of my strength, I gripped his arm and twisted hard. I didn't need to let him think he'd won anymore.

Lycus let go with a yelp like a wounded dog. I dropped to the concrete, my legs buckled beneath me. I sprawled there on all fours, gasping for breath.

Lycus let out an unearthly roar and turned towards me. His fingers grew unnaturally long, his fingernails curving once more into claws.

"Why don't you go get your cure?" I rasped. "You know, the one that's supposed to fix everything. Is that what Vic told you?"

"What…what have you done?" he cried. He doubled over, his cries of pain raising the hairs on my neck.

I stood up over him as he cowered at my feet and wiped sweat and spittle from my face. He looked up at me, his skin now waxy, unearthly. He reminded me strongly of the beast that attacked me my first day in the Shadowlands.

"I trusted the right person," I hissed at him. "You didn't."

I turned and walked back to the crawler, leaving him to the altered effects of Akrium. With one quick motion, I picked up the gun and climbed up onto the treads. Wes gripped me by the arm and started hauling me up towards the opening of the crawler.

"Get in!" he hollered. "We're going to blast through this mess!"

Working together, we scrambled up the metal sides of the massive vehicle and into the hole on the top. He hugged me close to him as we stood on the small platform beneath the hole, his heart beating so hard that I felt it through both our shirts.

"What's going on?" I asked.

"We've got to get down below," Wes replied. "We're going to set off a blast from the cannon on this thing. If it doesn't kill them, it'll at least make them scatter."

"You can't!" I hollered over the noise. "Those people…they used to be with the rebellion. They were injected against their will! They weren't even given the cure!"

Wes looked down and frowned. "I know, Lily. I don't like it any more than you do. But it's the only way to get through. It's either that or run them over. At least this way they get a warning."

I swallowed hard, choking on the ashy air. "But…"

"I know, Lily," Wes replied, "but look. Look at them."

I looked where he pointed and saw the maddened crowds pushing faster towards the crawler, some starting to climb up the treads. If they got in…well, I couldn't even think about it.

I allowed Wes to pull me down into the crawler and watched numbly as he twisted the hatch closed. Though we'd closed the top, the beasts still threw themselves at the machine. I heard them scrabbling with the door on the top, the hatch that would never open from the outside, and felt a surge of pity for them.

Wes and I sat down in the cramped space behind the driver's seat. I covered my ears and Wes held me as Conley readied the cannon. A loud blast echoed through the air, the power of the shot jerking the huge vehicle back. I caught my breath, acutely aware of ringing in my ears.

"We're clear," Conley called back grimly. I tried to shut out the sadness of his voice as the crawler rumbled forward towards the Mainframe, feeling glad that I couldn't see what he'd seen.

Chapter Thirty-One

"What do you reckon, Wes?" Conley shouted over the noise. "Blast our way in? Or send in a group?"

Wes looked to me. "Your call, Lily. I know you want to take the jerk down personally."

I felt like someone had handed me an unruly puppy and told me to figure out what to do with it. How could he just plunk this on me?

"I don't know," I replied, feeling very out of place. "All I know is I don't want mom going in there."

I was terrified for mom and wished now that we'd found a safe place for her to hide until this was all over.

"Who says I'm not coming in?" she protested from the back of the vehicle.

"I'm coming too," I chimed in Avery. "There's no way we can let you two or three go in alone."

Gradually our whole group nodded their assent. Whether it was the comfort in knowing that so many others stood behind us or just the sheer relief of knowing I wasn't alone, a plan suddenly formed in my mind.

"Okay," I began, "things will work best if we all stay together. A big group is much more intimidating than one or two people. My guess is he'll be in his office. Let's get in there, make sure everyone has a gun and tranquilizer bullets and take him down."

Everyone nodded. I moved my way back to mom and sat next to her.

"Stay with me no matter what," I whispered to her.

"Like I wouldn't," she replied, rolling her eyes.

"Seriously, mom." She frowned a little at the anxiety in my voice.

"Okay, honey, I will."

I gripped her hand and took a deep breath as Conely kept rolling the crawler through the city.

"I'm gonna take her right up to the front!" he hollered over the noise.

"Sounds good!" Wes yelled back. He looked at me and smiled briefly. I looked to my right and saw Levi glaring at Wes. A small sigh escaped me. Part of me wanted to finish this to be done with Vic forever, but the other part wanted even more to be done with this stupid love triangle.

All too soon, the crawler pulled right up to the doors. Wes and I climbed out, both of us with loaded rifles in hand, ready to catch anyone lingering by the doors, and clambered down the side of the massive vehicle. I circled the area by the massive front doors, checking for beasts, but no one seemed to be there. Wes thumped loudly with his fist on the metal siding of the crawler, signaling the others to open the back hatch so they could come out. Conley turned the machine off and crawled out last, clutching his rifle. Mom stood staring at her gun, clearly a little lost. I did my best to explain shooting to her, but without actual practice, I was more than a little nervous to see her with a weapon in her hands. Between the nine of us, only thirty bullets remained for the guns, enough for three each and a few left over.

Conley pushed the extra bullets into Wes's hands. "You two will probably be the ones to finish Channing off. You'll need them."

Wes took a deep breath and pocketed them. "Thanks, man."

All of us stood still for a few moments, trying to process what we were about to do. None of us had a clue what waited for us in the huge Mainframe building, but whatever it was couldn't be good. Knowing that someone had to take the lead, I gripped mom's hand with my free hand and started towards the glass double doors. They'd taken a beating in whatever had happened in the city. Shattered glass lay inside and outside the door, making me shudder. Without the glass in the panels, our group just stepped through the empty door frame.

The last time I'd been in the Mainframe, it had been a bustling place, filled with over-the-top extravagance and splendor. Now, the marble walls lay pockmarked from explosions. The fancy climbing plants lay shredded and unkempt. Chairs and tables and desks lay overturned. No one was in sight.

I held my breath and crept through the wreckage towards the elevator. Wes pushed the button, but nothing happened. He continued to jab at it until I suddenly realized the biggest difference in the Mainframe. The electricity was down. No lights, no power.

"There's no electricity, Wes," I pointed out, noticing that my breath came in small puffs. The air had grown abnormally cold for the city. It didn't help that the busted doors let the outside air in.

"No heat either," I continued. "Nothing's working in the building."

He backed up with a sigh, shouldering his gun. "Well…I guess it's the stairs, then."

"Shouldn't someone stay as guard if you're going up the stairs?" asked Levi, surprising me. He'd been silent since our last conversation at the docks in Epirus.

Wes narrowed his eyes. "Lily said we should all stick together."

"Yeah, but if we're climbing stairs and someone surprises us from behind, they have the upper hand," he argued back, his face pinching in anger. "It might be handy to have a rear guard. I can follow behind a little more slowly and catch anyone who might come up. It would be good to have a front guard-"

He stopped suddenly as a crashing sound reached our ears. A man, panting and foaming at the mouth, came raging through the broken doors. His eyes were wild, rolling in his head out of control. Deep growls and grunts came from him as he struggled over to us, his swollen head jerking back and forth irregularly. A loud blast sounded and the monster crumpled, gasping and growling in pain as the potent Akrium formula took effect.

I whirled around and saw Levi holding his rifle, the tip pointed at the savaged man.

"Told ya," he said with a shrug.

"Okay, he has a point," I offered, trying to make peace. "Levi, can you be our rear guard? I don't want you to stay on the first floor, but follow us slowly. Wes and I will take the front. The rest of you stay in the middle."

Everyone seemed to agree, though Wes remained tight-lipped and clearly angry. I took his hand and began searching for a stairwell, ensuring that mom stayed close behind me. We finally found the door to the stairs behind the wreckage of a massive marble fountain. I opened the door carefully, poking the barrel of my rifle inside first. No windows meant no light. Taking a deep breath, I stepped into the darkness of the stairwell and prayed that my eyes would adjust quickly.

The stairs wound upwards endlessly. We'd only reached the fourth floor before my legs and lungs burned in protest. No one had disturbed us or tried to stop us, but far from reassuring, the fact kept me on edge.

As we rounded the corner of the sixth floor staircase and approached the door, I stopped and put my hand out to warn the others. Footsteps.

I held my breath, trying to determine the direction. Before long, they were joined by more footsteps and low voices. Steeling myself, I peeked out of the door and looked both directions. To the right was a wall. To the left was a long hallway stretching into a dark nothingness. Rows of doors stood open along the corridor, and the stairs were to our rear.

I looked at Wes, sick to my stomach. They were coming towards us. We were trapped like rats.

"What do you want to do?" I asked as Wes peeked through the door.

"There's no one there right now," he concluded. "Let's try to get through one of these other doors and let them pass us."

I nodded and whispered to the others to follow us. We quickly herded everyone through the staircase door and into the hallway. I crept quietly into one of the rooms, gun aloft, and made a quick search. Empty.

I motioned the others in, counting heads. Suddenly, my heart froze.

Levi.

He must have gotten far behind us, still acting as rear guard. He wouldn't know about the people coming down the hall.

"I've got to find Levi," I whispered to Wes. He frowned deeply and shook his head.

"I'll go," he offered. "I don't want you getting caught."

"He won't come if it's you," I hissed, feeling an uncomfortable sense of urgency. Even if I didn't want to be with Levi romantically, he was still my friend. Wes started to protest, but I cut him off.

"You know I'm right," I said. "I'll be fine, don't worry."

I started to hurry off, but stopped as hurt showed plainly on Wes's face. I paused, then walked back and kissed him lightly, feeling really uncomfortable as everyone watched.

"I'll be back soon," I reassured him.

"You better," he replied, a hint of his old smile playing across his face.

I hurried off, my emotions mixing and churning in my head. The voices were definitely closer, but they were probably still far enough down the hall not to see me in the dark. A chill ran down my back as I noticed the beams of flashlights bouncing off the walls.

With a deep breath, I hurried back down the stairs, my legs cramping in protest. As I came tearing down the fifth floor staircase, I smacked right into Levi, who held his gun up in my face.

"It's me," I whispered frantically. "Levi, it's Lily."

"Oh," he replied with a sigh of relief. "Sorry about that."

I yanked on his arm. "We've got to get up the staircase. People are coming down the sixth floor hallway. We'll be trapped."

His eyes narrowed. "Since when do you care? I thought you'd be happy to have me out of the way. That's why I brought up a rear guard in the first place, so I wouldn't have to burden you with my presence."

"Oh, would you quit with your little pity party?" I snapped. "I came back because you're my friend, and you've saved me from tight places more than I care to admit. I can't believe you'd think I could be so heartless as to not return the favor."

I started to head up the stairs. "Let's go!"

"I'm sorry," he muttered.

I turned to see, to my chagrin, that he hadn't moved. "Levi, we have to *go!*"

He still didn't move, so I crept down the stairs to where he stood. I stepped back when I noticed tears in his eyes. He turned away and swiped his hand over his face, scowling.

"Look," I said softly, "I'm sorry too."

I touched his arm and suddenly wished I hadn't. I felt a surge of regret, wondering if I'd written him off too soon. Then again, I couldn't ever write off Wes. It suddenly occurred to me that I hadn't been fair. To either of them.

"Levi, I care about you. A lot." I took a deep breath. "More than I should."

He looked at me, trying to make his face hard and unfeeling, but not succeeding.

"But I love Wes."

"Yeah, yeah, Lily, I know," he shot back.

He turned around and smacked the wall with his hand, making a loud clang. I grabbed him by the arm and pulled him back.

"Knock it off!" I murmured. "You want the whole lot of them on us?"

"They're not even close," he scoffed, cradling his hand.

"Look, I'm sorry that I hurt and misled you. I didn't mean to, okay? But if we don't get out of here now, it'll be you and me against a huge bunch of thugs. Let's get through this, let's end this stupid war and then we'll figure things out!"

Finally, he moved. We headed back up the stairs, but I could see flashlights bobbing over the walls above us.

"Move down!" I whispered. "They're coming this way!"

We got down to the next hall and found an empty room. Levi dove under an overturned desk and pulled me down with him. Footsteps sounded on the stairs, in the hall, outside the door of our hiding spot.

"I thought I heard something around here," came a nasaly voice from the hall.

"You're probably hearing rats," said another voice, sounding tired. "Let's just get back to the first floor. Vic's orders, right?"

I noticed they sounded a little annoyed about taking "Vic's orders," and my hammering heart rose a few notches. If a big group of guards were being sent to the first floor, maybe we had a chance to go on without being seen. Vic wouldn't be stupid enough to send all of his guards to the first floor, but perhaps there wouldn't be as many. The footsteps receded down the stairs, moving quickly by the sound of it.

"Let's go," I whispered, taking Levi by the arm.

We scurried quietly out of the room, looked both ways, then hurried up the stairs. A paralyzing fear gripped me as the same nasaly voice we'd heard suddenly barked down at us.

"Well, well…looks like Vic was right."

There had been footsteps, all right, but one going up and one going down. I bit my lip hard, feeling stupid for making such a careless mistake.

I looked up slowly, dread filling my heart. A beast stood above us on the stairs, grinning eerily down at us.

Chapter Thirty-Two

I moaned desparingly, hoping Levi couldn't hear me. I could definitely take on people who hadn't been injected with Akrium at all, but taking on a full-fledged beast was something else altogether. I remembered that I still gripped a gun and raised it warily, knowing he'd be on me if I even tried to load a bullet.

"I was hoping I'd be the one to bring you to Vic," sneered the beast, a sickening grin playing across his pale face. "You're quite the incentive. Bring Lily to Vic, and you get a cure."

He laughed a little, a creepy laugh that made him sound insane. I swallowed hard, feeling my hands shaking on the gun.

"I knew you were here," he continued. "You see, different senses are developed and heightened when you become a beast. Mine happened to be hearing."

An odd curiosity struck me then. I'd never heard that about Akrium. I always thought it just gave you super strength.

"I heard you and your little pals. Where are they?" he taunted. "You can tell me, or we can play cat and mouse. The cat has a grenade, though, so I don't think the mouse has much of a chance…"

He held up the small grenade and snickered horribly, insanely. My mind raced, trying to find an answer, a way out of this, but to no avail.

"You don't have to do this," I said lamely. "We have a cure. We'll fix you without any price. You can have it for free. Just do the right thing."

I sounded stupid, even to myself. The man scoffed.

"Yeah, like that's any kind of guarantee," he jeered. His finger reached for the pin. "Here, mousy mousy mousy…"

"Why don't you get off your butt and look for us yourselves?"

The beast suddenly slumped, his head twisted back at an odd angle. Wes stood behind him, the butt of his gun raised. I grabbed the grenade that fell from his hand and stuffed it in my pocket after ensuring the pin was still inside the device. Wes slammed down on the beasts' head with the butt of his gun one more time, but the beast was up on his feet in a flash. I fumbled in my pocket for more ammo, and stuffed a bullet into the barrel with shaking hands. Wes struggled with the psycho, pushing against him with all his strength, trying to get him to the stairs. I dropped my gun, realizing what he was doing, and ran to help him. Levi, seeming to read my mind, came up the stairs beside me.

"On three," I muttered to him. "One, two…"

"Three," he finished as we came level with the beast. Both of us reached out for one of the beasts' legs. His body slammed heavily down on the tile floor. Levi and I yanked him back and sent him tumbling down the long staircase. I followed a few steps, took careful aim, and shot. The tranquilizer hit the beast square in the back as he tumbled down. I whirled around and scurried up the stairs.

"Move! Up to the penthouse!" I shouted to Wes and the others. They didn't pause to ask questions. As one, we thundered desperately up the stairs, no longer taking care to be quiet. The clatter the beast had raised on the stairs had surely alerted everyone in the building.

By the fifteenth floor, most of us were completely worn out. None of us could run anymore, and even my breaths were becoming haggard gasps.

"We've got to find somewhere secure for mom and the scientists," I panted. "They need to hide. We can't just keep climbing like this in a huge group."

Wes nodded, still struggling to catch his breath. "Vic's on the twenty-fifth floor. We'll probably run into a lot more beasts on our way up there."

"Let's hide the others on this floor, then. It's almost in the middle," I decided. Knowing beasts would probably search rooms and offices, I found an out-of-the-way storage closet and put mom and the scientists in there.

"Lily, you can't do this! I'm not letting you go up there alone!" she protested.

"Mom, I can't risk you getting hurt," I replied, avoiding her pleading gaze. "I'll be fine. Wes and the others will protect me."

I turned to Johnson.

"Protect her with your life. If anything happens to her, I'll kill you," I told him. His eyebrows shot up in surprise and fear. I shouldered my gun and shrugged.

"Just kidding," I amended as I turned towards the hall. "Sort of."

He laughed a little, then patted my arm.

"She's safe with us," he promised.

I nodded, too choked up to talk anymore. I hugged mom, holding her more tightly than I probably should have, and walked briskly away. Wes shut and secured the door, surrounding it with debris to make it look like it hadn't been disturbed.

We made it four more floors before we encountered another beast. True to his word, Trent had created a formula that worked fast. We felled three more beasts on our way up, using the same technique we'd used on the first beast. I was surprised that we hadn't met more, but worried that it meant we'd meet several on the top floor.

The penthouse floor finally came into view. We struggled up the last few steps and collapsed on the landing, totally exhausted and covered in sweat. My heart sank a little, wondering how we'd be able to fight in this condition.

I didn't have long to wonder. Whether we were ready or not, the flood of beasts came with a vengeance. Wes helped me up, and all of us loaded the last few bullets we had. After that, I didn't know what would come.

Twenty or so beasts came rushing at us all at once, making my heart pound loudly in my ears.

"Shoot on my signal," gasped Wes as the psychotic hordes charged down the hallway towards us.

He held up his hand, waiting, waiting for what felt like an eternity. Finally, it came down and all four of us fired at once. A quick reload, and another wave of beasts fell. Another reload, another wave of beasts gone. The process continued until we'd exhausted all our bullets and the extras from the others' guns.

I closed my eyes and focused my anger, pain, fear and fatigue into one spot in my mind, letting my rage explode over me. With an unholy roar, I rushed the remaining five or so beasts, my fist connecting immediately with the first beast's face. His nose broke with a satisfying crunch. I saw the others around me, smacking heads with the butts of the rifles, darting here and there, trying to avoid the claws of the beasts. I jumped high with my leg out, my foot connecting with another beast's chest.

Wes cried out suddenly and hunched down, holding his arm. A beast had slashed him with his claws.

"NO!" I roared, so angry I could barely see. I strode over to the beast and slammed him against the wall. With another feral cry, I lifted him bodily and

- 166 -

carried him to the stairs where I threw him down. I rushed back to the scene to see one beast still resiliently fighting Avery and Levi.

"Move out of the way!" I hollered, not even recognizing my own voice. They obeyed quickly, looking scared at the sight of me. I lowered my head and charged, my shoulder making contact with the beasts' soft middle. He grunted, but I didn't give him the chance to recover. My fists came up next, pushing as much force as I could against his nose. He crumpled, nose bleeding. With a wild scream, I kicked his ribs, knowing they would be broken.

I stood up and wiped my nose, realizing for the first time that it was bleeding. My breaths came in heaving gasps that shook my whole body. The force of the adrenaline began to make me dizzy.

"Lily, what's going on?" asked Avery as she rushed to my side. I fell back. She caught me and laid me down gently. Wes rushed over, still cradling his arm. Levi soon joined them, a large gash on his forehead.

"I...I don't know," I whispered faintly. "This has never happened to me before."

I took stock of myself. I still breathed painfully, but the only place bleeding was my nose. My head felt as if it had been beaten with a baseball bat.

"Oh my-"

Avery cut herself off when she pressed her hand hard against her lips.

"Lily...your leg..." said Levi, pointing.

I looked towards where he stared and gasped in horror. Rooted in my leg, in the soft flesh of my calf just above the ankle, was one of the large tranquilizer bullets. The pointed metal tip had dug in deeply, and some of the vile liquid still remained, pumping even now into my bloodstream.

Chapter Thirty-Three

"What happened?" Wes asked, his face very pale, his lips shaking as he talked.

"I don't know," I whispered. "Maybe it was in my pocket or something…"

The bullets were more like darts, designed to get the Akrium formula into the bloodstream as fast as possible. My mind raced, wondering how the formula would cope with a body like mine. Then, realizing that Trent had designed them for people who had been cured to my level, my heart sank.

A harsh, raspy laugh sounded behind us. I turned to see a beast lying on his stomach, clearly in pain, but grinning horribly.

"Thought you were invincible, eh girl? Well, one good turn deserves another," he snarled, the vicious grin twisting into a look of pure hatred. Wes smacked him hard with the butt of a rifle and the beast slumped, unmoving.

"We've got to get to a train or something," Wes panted. "We've got to get her to a cure."

"Think about what you're saying, Wes," Avery interrupted. "We're at the top of the biggest building in the city. There's no way we can get down out of here in time."

"We have to do something!" he screamed, his face twisted with pain and anger. I felt strangely surreal as I watched everything around me. Time seemed to have slowed down, making things look and feel as if they were underwater. I closed my eyes, trying my best to wade through the confusion in my brain.

"Stop," I panted wearily. "Just stop."

Wes and Avery fell silent.

"Our first priority," I wheezed, "is to kill Vic. Kill him, and the war is over."

Without waiting for help, I stood up and gripped the end of the tranquilizer. With a grunt of pain, I wrenched it from my leg.

"What are you *doing*?" shouted Levi.

Ignoring him, I pushed past them towards the office. The golden doors had been slightly bent off of their hinges. I summoned another burst of strength and pushed through them. The others followed hastily in my wake.

"About time, Miss Mitchell. I was starting to get worried."

Vic turned from the massive windows that overlooked the city, his usual glass of whiskey tightly clutched in his clawed hand. He looked far different from what I'd remembered, though. I gasped slightly as I noticed his swollen head, yellow skin stretched tightly over his skull, now bare of its former greasy patch. Flashing red eyes peered fiercely at me.

"You watch the destruction of your city and have a drink while you do it?" I spat, feeling anger surge through me, dulling the pain slightly.

"I didn't cause this destruction. You did," he replied simply. "You have no idea what it's like to have a starving country on your hands, Miss Mitchell, but if you had some inkling, you'd have given yourself to research long ago as you were supposed to."

"I am not some science project!" I screamed. "I never wanted or deserved any of this! I refuse to be some pawn in your little game!"

He laughed jeeringly, then threw the glass of whiskey at the window in a sudden fit of anger. His face turned bright red as he turned to face me.

"It is not for you to decide your fate, *Lily*," he hissed. "Those who honor their country know their place, even if it means giving their lives. Your one life could have saved many, but you were too selfish to see that!"

"Talk about selfish! You're the king of selfishness!" I yelled, feeling the anger beginning to pulse inside me again. "We're all starving, so let's invade the south and kill innocent people! Let's inject thousands of people with a volatile chemical and see if anything changes! Let's deprive a dying woman of her daughter, her only caretaker, just so we can have the glory of wiping out another country!"

"You don't know what you're talking about!" he shot back. "If you had any pride in your country, as do I, you would pay any price to save it! I've given my own life to save it! I've become this," he gestured to himself, "in order to try and salvage what's left of the city after your little rebellion got through with it!"

He paused for a few deep breaths, his chest heaving, his red eyes staring at me hatefully. All at once, a startling realization hit me. He'd really believed that he was doing the right thing. He'd really believed he was only trying to save his country. For a moment, I felt unsure of everything I believed I'd been fighting for, but it passed quickly. Vic may have had noble intentions at some point, but he sure wasn't choosing a noble way to fix the problem. He was insane with power.

"Yes, I had the cure from that fool Lycus," he sneered, "but it was only a temporary fix. We needed subsequent treatments to eradicate the poisoning completely. Supplies ran out. Nobody knew how to replicate it. And now, here I am."

He grabbed the bottle of whiskey on his table and took a long, full drink straight from the bottle, wiping his mouth with his filthy sleeve. With a glare of hatred aimed at me, he picked up a small pistol.

"I'm not much longer for this world," he muttered, "but I can still have the pleasure of killing you and everyone you care about, Mitchell."

He raised the gun, and everything slowed down. I felt each breath rising in my chest, knowing suddenly that they would be my last. Vic pulled the trigger and a loud bang echoed through the room.

"No!" came a shout from somewhere to my left. Something slammed heavily into me, pushing me aside. I looked over my shoulder and saw, to my horror, that Levi had pushed me out of the bullets' path. He crumpled slowly to the floor, red blossoming from his chest.

I felt as if someone had punched me in the neck. No matter how hard I tried, I couldn't draw breath.

"Levi!" I gasped, kneeling next to him.

"You've got to be kidding me!" raged Vic. I turned to see him readying another shot. Something like a mini-explosion occurred inside me. I hurled to my feet and charged after Vic, swiping the gun out of his hand. Mustering my last ounce of super-human strength, I lifted Vic by the shirt, off his feet and threw him forcefully at the glass panes of the massive windows. The glass shattered into a thousand shards as Vic screamed. His body seemed to levitate for a moment before falling through the sky, out of view.

Without a second thought, I ran to Levi and cradled his head in my arms. He breathed shallowly, his face pale and drawn. I didn't want to see the wound in his chest. I knew without seeing that he was gone.

"I'm so sorry," I sobbed, wishing I didn't sound so stupid and useless. "I…I should have died instead of you."

"No, Lily," he said, running his fingers gently through my hair. "No. You have a life to live. You have great things to do. Now you can do them," he whispered.

"I can't live without you," I replied, realizing how much I really had grown to care for him. "I…I love you."

He smiled, the first real smile I'd ever seen on his face. "Then everything is okay," he said. "I love you too, Lily. You're the best friend I've ever had."

I buried my face in his shoulder, the sobs coming hard and fast. Guilt paralyzed me, making me feel like I would never be worth anything, ever.

His breathing quickened. I lifted my head to look in his eyes one last time, and, on a sudden impulse, kissed him. As I pulled away, his smile widened. He winked at me before his haunting, dark eyes closed forever.

My heart exploded into a million pieces. I sat beside Levi, unable to will myself to move. I just stared at him, holding his hand, wishing that he would wake up and everything would be okay again.

At some point, Wes crouched beside me. I looked up at him and saw with a shock that there was no trace of jealousy or spite on his face. Tears ran gently down his cheeks.

"Don't let his sacrifice go in vain," he said gently. "We need to get you to the others. Johnson and Robertson will know what to do."

Part of me wanted to protest, to say that I'd rather die than go on living with this guilt. But in the end, I knew he was right. Levi had died so that I could live. I couldn't just sit here forever and give up.

"Yeah," I replied slowly. I let Wes take me softly by the arm and lift me up. Some of the ache eased as he gathered me into his arms and held me tight.

"I'm so sorry, Lily. He was…he was a really good guy." Wes's voice was thick with emotion, and I realized that somewhere along the way, they must have made peace with each other.

Wes and Avery hurriedly created a makeshift stretcher from a curtain hanging on the wall. They carefully rolled Levi's body onto the curtain, rolled it gently around him like a hammock, and lifted him slowly.

It seemed hours before we finally got to the fifteenth floor where we'd left mom and the scientists. Angling Levi's body down the stairs had taken more strength than we possibly had left, but all of us refused to leave him behind.

"Lily!" mom cried out when we pried open the door to the storage closet. She wrapped me in her arms and I tried to hug her back, but everything felt so numb, so unreal. I tried to smile bravely, but my bravado evaporated as she began to cry over Levi.

"We need to get Lily a cure," Wes said urgently to Johnson. "She got injected with a dart."

Johnson looked at me doubtfully, then leaned in towards Wes, whispering in his ear. I knew without hearing that getting a cure looked pretty hopeless. I'm sure he remembered how to do it, but finding supplies was another matter completely. I turned away, no longer caring about anything, least of all my own life.

Chapter Thirty-Four

"We will never forget the great sacrifice of this man," said Wes. "It is to him that I owe my life, and the life of Lily Mitchell, and Avery Donovan. May he rest in peace."

I stared down at the small, crude wooden box being lowered into the ground, no longer numb, but sobbing freely.

We'd somehow made it to some kind of laboratory at one of the government offices in the city, though the events of the last few days remained a dull haze in my mind. Johnson and Robertson had managed to rummage through the remains of the lab and found the necessary ingredients for a cure. They'd cured me, and predictably, my body responded well to the treatment. I healed very quickly. They'd then found a few more of their fellow scientists and made it their mission to cure anyone who'd been injected.

We traveled north from there and buried Levi close to the ocean on the cliffs, so that even in death, he could look out at the waves. I missed him horribly even now, even in the aftermath of the war. I didn't know how things would ever be the same again. Part of me didn't want to think about it. That part of me wanted to hunker down and give up, never talking to or interacting with anyone ever again. But the other part of me, the part that remembered Levi's sacrifice for what it was, kept me going. I needed to live my life, the way he would have wanted me to. I couldn't give up.

After the small funeral, Wes stepped over to me and reached for my hand. He'd been so good to me, so understanding. He didn't kiss or touch me as much as I knew he wanted to, and I was grateful. It was hard to sort out exactly what I was feeling. I loved Wes more than ever, and knew that I always would, but a part of my heart would always belong to Levi.

Wes started to walk away, but I grabbed him gently by the arm and pulled him back. I kissed him lightly on the lips, the first time since the horrible things that happened at the Mainframe. He smiled a bit, then frowned, trying not to look too happy.

"It's okay, Wes. I think Levi knew that no matter what, you and I would end up together. He wanted it this way in the end, I think." I took his hand, suddenly not wanting to talk anymore.

He smiled half-heartedly. "I hope you know that even below all his bull-headedness, I really did appreciate him. I meant every word I said, and I'm glad that the two of you met."

I smiled back. "Me too. And thank you for the eulogy. It was beautiful."

"No problem." He gave my hand an extra squeeze, then walked towards the others still gathered around the burial site. I walked a ways off, not ready to face people other than mom, Wes and Avery just yet. I sat down on the edge of the cliff, staring out at the beautifully calm water reflecting the sun. The pure blue sky didn't have even a trace of cloud. Though it was still chilly, being the middle of January, I thought the weather was a perfect tribute to Levi.

I took the quiet moment to reflect on things. Arduba was under repair. The entire population of the city had banded together, making an effort to clean up the streets and clear out the rubble. The Mainframe had been torn down, and in its place, a newer and less imposing building was under construction. George had been chosen as the new president by a unanimous vote of those who remained alive. Being from the north, a first for the president of Illyria, he had the right connections and relations to solve the food problem.

George had also effectively arranged a peace treaty with Epirus, though relations were still a bit testy. Conley had come up for Levi's funeral, then planned to go back to Epirus and continue peace talks with the government there. He'd been made the ambassador to Illyria.

After extensive talks and debates, the remaining stores of Akrium and treatments that Trent had developed had been locked in a large, leak-proof safe and dumped far out to sea, in the hopes that future generations wouldn't get hold of it and misuse it as we had. The Akrium mines were shut down, bombed and condemned, sealed off and guarded round the clock with capitol soldiers. With everyone cured, hope prevailed. The world finally began to make sense again.

And I hoped it would stay that way.

Epilogue

Five Years Later

As we walked along the beach, Wes gently took my hand. I smiled at him, still feeling the old thrill that his touch had always given me.

"Come on, ladies, keep up!" he called back behind his shoulder. Tears rose to my eyes as I turned back and watched mom cradling our nine-month-old daughter, Danielle, in her arms as they waded in the surf. Mom's face lit up with delight as Dani giggled at the splashing water. I studied my little girl fondly, so amazed to see Wes's eyes in her little face, to see wisps of my wavy hair beginning on her head. I wondered vaguely if she had inherited my freak powers. Given how hard she could squeeze my hand, the odds were good.

"We're coming," mom called. "She sure likes the water, just like her mother."

Mom smiled at me, the special smile she reserved only for me, and her worn face suddenly looked years younger. I smiled back, feeling my throat tighten once again. I couldn't remember ever being so happy in my whole life.

My happiness went down a notch as the strange, old church came into view. Mom caught up with us, her smile replaced by an unreadable expression.

"He's just around the back, mom," I said softly, taking hold of her free hand. All of us fell silent as we rounded the old church and came to the roughly-made stone markers. I led her to the one marked "Mitchell."

Mom's grasp tightened on my hand. I squeezed back, tears forming in my eyes. We stood there for a long time, gazing down at my father's grave. Wes's arm slipped around my shoulders.

"I never thought I'd see his grave," mom whispered. "I never knew someone buried him. For all I knew, he was lost to me forever."

I wrapped my arm around her shoulders and the three of us stood there, holding each other, wrapped in the silence of the moment.

It had taken five years and a ton of research, but I'd finally managed to get an old sea-chart from the Illyria Ocean Patrol, showing the location of the island Avery and I had found so many years ago. I knew I couldn't just let the memory fade, never giving mom the chance to see dad again, so I'd convinced her to come out here with us to pay our last respects. The look on her face told me I'd done the right thing.

After a while, we left. A strange mixture of sadness and peace fell over me as we walked away from the old church, from dad's final resting place. Mom wrapped her arm around my waist and let it lay there until we reached the shore and climbed into our rented boat.

As we drove toward Lander's Beach, I reflected about how much things had changed in the past five years since the end of the war. The capitol looked brighter, cleaner and more prosperous than I'd ever seen it. Avery had gotten a position working with the government as a plant specialist. Her knowledge of herbs came in handy not only in cleansing the soil from the effects of the Burial, but also in medicine and other technology. She thrived in her job, feeling as if it truly was her calling. We still visited her occasionally. She especially loved to see Dani.

George had tried to retire as president a year ago, but was elected to another term by popular demand. Illyria thrived under his guiding hand. The crops had grown every year without fail, ending our food shortage. Relations with Epirus had eased as well, and the two countries had become great allies. Illyria provided Epirus with much needed weapons technology to protect them from other nations that would seek to invade, and Epirus provided further knowledge of how to grow food and store it properly against another disaster. Conley and his wife came up every now and again to celebrate holidays or other special occasions with our family. They'd become fast friends.

Wes's knowledge of communications had landed him a job up at the Communications Department in Parthin. We lived now in a small house on the coast, near the beaches I loved so much. This excursion was our first trip back to the capitol since the end of the war.

The sun set over the ocean, casting everything in a soft, orange glow. I breathed in the salty air and let my tense shoulders relax. I had to remind myself often that the war was over, that we were free, and that life would go on.

Acknowledgements

I can't believe Shadowlands is already done. From my first germ of an idea six years ago to now, I have grown to love these characters.

Shadowlands is my first published trilogy, and I am immensely excited to have reached this landmark as a writer. I have always wanted to write a series of novels, and now I can say I did!

Though I work mostly alone in these projects, I have several people to thank. First, to my husband Chris, who is my faithful fact-checker, someone I can run my ideas by, and an honest evaluator of how the story should be shaped. Next, to all the wonderful musicians out there who inspire me with their music. It is very hard to write or imagine things without music. My hat is off to all you super creative people. I'm thankful to Amazon who made it possible to publish my book without having to wait around forever to get a form letter from a publisher. My dream has come true thanks to this innovative new technology that allows me to bypass the middleman. And no, they didn't pay me to say that. As in my dedication, I'm grateful for wonderful parents who fostered my imagination. I'm incredibly thankful for devoted educators who encouraged me to pursue a writing career. And I'm thankful for family and friends who have worked hard to promote this series through various social media outlets. And finally, thank you Voltaire, for lending me such an awesome quote that matched so perfectly with this story.

Brittiany West is a published author of several short stories and now four novels. She holds a Bachelor of Art Degree in English with an emphasis in Creative Writing. Mrs. West lives with her husband and five children in Ohio.

Printed in Great Britain
by Amazon.co.uk, Ltd.,
Marston Gate.